# HEART OF A VAMPIRE

While Lamia Zacharius gave the appearance always of rare, haughty beauty and a serene, sophisticated kind of self-control, there remained in her private heart some final traces of the poor, slight, wide-eyed child she had once been in the streets of ancient Greece—an orphan, hungrier more times than not, starved for affection and kind words. Perhaps this is why she hungered now for her forays to be more than mere vampirization, to prove mutually fulfilling, and they so seldom were.

Occasionally, however, there was that sensitive, perceptive male victim who managed to look her in the eyes with gratitude at the moment she tore out his throat to feast. These were the times that made everything worthwhile. And this particular evening, as she tiptoed through the house and drifted like a slender shadow into the early-winter darkness, she hoped this would prove to be a night to remember. . . .

# READ THESE HORRIFYING BEST SELLERS!

# DEATH-ANGEL

## BY J.N. WILLIAMSON

**ZEBRA BOOKS**
**KENSINGTON PUBLISHING CORP.**

ZEBRA BOOKS

are published by

KENSINGTON PUBLISHING CORP.
475 Park Avenue South
New York, N.Y. 10016

Printed in the United States of America

*For the women who are, were, or will be appreciated: Mary, my wife and agent; my daughter Mary; my sister Marylynn; Nancy R. Parsegian; Jane Thornton; Leslie Gelbman; Cathryn Gibson: Spouse! Sister! Angel! Pilot of the Fate Whose course has been so starless! . . . Thy wisdom speaks in me, and bids me dare Beacon the rocks on which high hearts are wrecked.*

A deadly silence step by step increased,
Until it seem'd a horrid presence there.
And not a man but felt the terror in his hair.
*"Lamia!"* he shrieked; and nothing but
    the shriek
With its sad echo did the silence break.
"Begone, foul dream!" he cried . . .
                    —John Keats, *Lamia*


Who waits but till the destined hour
    arrive,
Bearing from *Demogorgon's* vacant throne
The dreadful might of ever-living limbs
Which clothed that awful spirit unbeheld,
To redescend, and trample out the spark.

'Tis the vintage-time for death and sin:
Blood, like new wine, bubbles within:
    Till Despair smothers
The struggling world.
                    —Percy B. Shelley
                    *Prometheus Unbound*

Horrible forms,
What and who are ye? Never yet there
        came
Phantasms so foul through monster-
        teeming Hell . . .
                —Shelley, *Prometheus Unbound*

For that she was a woman, and without
Any more subtle fluid in her veins
Than throbbing *blood* . . .
                —Keats, *Lamia*

## PROLOGUE

Peter Plagjowicz, one of the Polish Upirs, terrified his fellow citizens of the small village named
Kisilova—terrified, manipulated, commanded and
slaughtered them for more than a year. Then, he
died.

Or seemed to.

Opening his grave as the sun began to rise,
tight-lipped with the intention of destroying his

body, the surviving villagers gaped when they saw how pink-cheeked and fresh of face Peter was. His nails—"*Look!*" cried the gravedigger, pointing, "Look at his *nails!*"—had continued to grow. It seemed apparent that the dirt in his grave nurtured Peter, that death itself agreed with him.

It was when they *pinched* those fat pink cheeks, and blobs of blood seeped from the pucker of his carmine lips that most of them turned away in horror. One, who knew what to do, suggested fetching a stake and a mallet . . .

Peter Plagjowicz was a pace setter, of sorts, a leader. He was history's first famous vampire. No one who knew him in life or in death would have quarreled with his right to the designation. A worse fate awaited Arnold Paul.

It was the Year of Our Lord 1730; the locale was the Turco-Serbian border. There dwelled a middle aged man whom many said was superstitious. Good hearted, but plagued by awful notions without a *soupcón* of common sense or reality. Arnold was a family man who worked hard and went regularly to church. He loved his wife and family and he believed, down to the homemade shoes on his rather large feet, that a vampire was out to get him.

It happened that the Turks and Serbians knew little of Polish legend and were unacquainted with the story of Peter Plagjowicz. For that matter, Arnold Paul knew nothing of history's first

8

vampire; he only knew that a curse lay on his head and that it specified his eventual demise and regeneration, as a vampire. Freud hadn't been born yet and none of the townspeople knew anything about psychology. A man was either sane or crazy; he told the truth or he lied. Some of them, who had found their sheep or cattle drained of blood, wondered if Arnold could be right and the majority of them believed he was crazy. The clergyman who tried to dissuade Arnold from his beliefs wound up halfway convinced himself that something creeping, shadowed and evil lurked in the village, and rather wished he hadn't brought the issue up at all.

"Have you ever *seen* a vampire?" asked Mrs. Paul, vigorously stirring a large-handled spoon in a pot as she spoke. "Have you ever known one?"

"No," Arnold replied. "But you've heard the rumors about the highwaymen buried at the edge of town. Everybody knows *they* were vampires."

She paused, turning her plain face to study her husband. "What do you plan to do about it? I mean, if you're sure about it, shouldn't you have some kind of amulet to protect you?"

"Alas, I know no one who makes such things," he said sadly. "The last witch in town was stoned to death. However," he continued, brightening, "I do have a way of guarding against the vampire bite."

"A relief," she breathed, "it's a relief to know

it. What way?"

"Upon the day when the vampire finally apprehends me, I will drop to my knees before his grave."

"How manly," Mrs. Paul observed dryly. "What then?"

"I will fill my mouth with earth from his grave." Arnold smiled and kissed the back of her leathery neck. "Everyone knows a vampire cannot kill someone who consumes the dirt of his grave."

"Lie down till supper's ready," she advised him in wifely tones. "Perhaps this will pass."

Several weeks went by, summer died horribly, and it was late October and willful winds whistled through the bare-boned structures of the village. The sharp threat of early winter sounded in every squalling tone, echoing along the floorboards of the houses and snuffling like mad invisible dogs. Shingles on Arnold Paul's aging roof tentatively flapped and rose, like the wings of trapped birds as he clucked encouragingly at his horses and coaxed his haywagon into the dusty road. His family depended on this delivery, and Arnold put thoughts of vampire-lust out of his mind to prod the horses forward.

Near the edge of town, however, a sliver-thin red fox darted out from the weeds and Arnold's haggard steeds reared, ears laid back and eyes wild with terror. The wagon was toppled at once and

Arnold thrown clear.

He might have been luckier if he'd been instantly killed. Instead, Arnold came to his senses with the realization that he'd been unceremoniously tossed atop the gravesite of the vampire highwaymen he had discussed with his wife. Dazed, unable to rise, Arnold Paul was unable to dine on dirt and became a meal, of sorts, himself, as the evil of the undead seeped from the mound into every shrinking pore of his body.

His worst fears and prophecy, his terrible, inhuman destiny, was fulfilled. Within days, ordinary Arnold Paul became the most awesome and malicious vampire on the Turco-Serbian border, raping women, plundering the other farmers, biting the heads off chickens, and generally making a nuisance of himself.

That much of the story was handed down from generation to generation. How much of it is rumor, distorted by the telling and retelling, one cannot with certainty say. The rest, however, was recorded when it occurred and was attested to by several townspeople who signed their names or made their marks and verified the story of Arnold Paul for all time to come.

One dark and wintry night, two months later, when shreds of snow clung to the fields like false crops shoved up from beneath the surface of the hard-packed ground, the arch vampire Arnold slew so many people in one ghoulish night that he

11

died of the shock. The villagers, of course, rejoiced; they were overcome with joy. "We are free of the monster," they shouted, "free of his terror by night!"

Yet there were those who knew much remained to be done before safety was truly restored. The mayor read books. He was a wise man who knew that, forty days after Arnold's passing, it would be their task to exhume his coffin and . . . do things . . . to the body.

Thus it was that in mid-February at the appropriate moment of midnight, the mayor, local clergymen, and other brave and learned souls went forth to perform the requisite chore. It is to their credit that they did not look forward to it, nor that they shrank from the job. Good Christians shouldered their duty and let it lead them to the worksite, even if it turned out to be a grim, forbidding grave in the loneliest part of the cemetery. The unblessed, unhallowed portion of the cemetery.

Because the gravedigger had packed the ground in hard, forty days ago, personally determined that nothing would escape from a grave *he* had dug and filled, and because the ground had frozen with the crushing tide of winter, it took the valiant little band more than an hour to reach the casket. Fat, steady-falling globules of snow slyly covered their backs yet melted from the perspiration rising through their winter garments. Still everyone was breathing hard, turning the air in the deep grave to vapors of steam when the burly gravedigger put out his trembling hand, clutched, and lifted. Creaking, the coffin lid was raised.

Arnold Paul looked soberly up at them, his eyes red and comatose, but wide open and somehow . . . *alive*. The expression on his face was disdainful, as if it said to them all *see, I told you!* Even worse, blood still bubbled in his veins so energetically that it appeared to ooze from the pores of Arnold's pallid skin. His entire body was sheathed in a shroud of stinking crimson. Beyond those who gaped and froze, the bailiff, knowing they were prepared, firmly shouted the foreordained order: "Pierce his heart!"

Instantly the mayor overcame his horror and gripped the stake, the point down. Beside him the balding, sallow-skinned clergyman raised the hammer threateningly above Arnold's wildly-beating, satyr's heart. Then, like an avenging scythe, the heavy tool swept the air, and plunged deep into Arnold's torso.

*At the moment of impact, it is written, the viable, vile corpse of Arnold Paul burst into flames and, showering the red scraps of his body in all directions, exploded. The noise caused homes to reverberate, horses miles away whinnied in fear, and those who were struck by the flying segments of the late Mr. Paul were forever marked by the scorched in scar of an upside-down cross.*

The people of Poland, the descendants of those who resided on the Turco-Serbian border and the villagers in Yugoslavia and Czechoslovakia and many other nations where science does not dominate their private senses say vampires existed. Because they cannot truly die, they continue to exist, as indestructible as St. Nicholas, Sherlock Holmes, and D'Artagnan. In more modern locations, of course, the facts are disputed. People pretend they no longer believe, they tell *everyone* they no longer believe. Only in the solitude of their own longer, darker nights when stealthy shadows rise from nothing and earth sounds betray the movement of unseen things in long-forgotten caskets do these modern people cross themselves, drink coffee, swallow tranquilizers, or remember how long it's been since they last spoke with Mom and Dad.

Is that the real reason why vampires still exist?

If so, what is one to make of vampires who are *not* unwanted men from the superstitious village nor even advanced, evil male creatures peering surreptitiously from beneath great, swinging cloaks?

What happens when they are *women*; incredibly beautiful, sensual, psychic women, like Lamia Zacharius?

What then?

The first "great initiate" of recorded history, Pythagoras . . . He wanted to understand the world because he believed that its principles were basically mystical or occult. We may note, in passing, that the Greeks seem to have lived to a greater age than most races."

—Colin Wilson, *The Occult*

Whither fled Lamia, now a lady bright,
A full-born beauty new and exquisite?
. . . There she stood
About a young bird's flutter from a
    wood . . .
To see herself escap'd from so sore ills,
While her robes flaunted with the
    daffodils.

"I have no friends," said Lamia, "no,
    not one . . . !"

—Keats, *Lamia*

# I

Dying, after three-thousand years of magically-prolonged life, seemed utterly pointless, even simple-minded, to beautiful Lamia Zacharius.

It wasn't a snap decision. At times, she'd really believed she might go through with it and see what death was like. Still in the temporary guise of pretty, teen-aged Lythia for days before her brothers and sisters of Thessaly, Indiana, marched bravely to certain death at the insistence of their eternal leader Pythagoras, the dark-haired vampire queen had appraised the depth of her loyalty.

True, they had all adored and admired the old man, even in his most recent incarnation as the jolly town leader Milo Traphonius. It was he who had summoned them to the Hoosier state and commanded them to build a town in preparation for the end of the world. Months ahead of time, Pythagoras had revealed the terrible truth written in *Logos*, his mentor Empedocles' ancient book of world prophecy, and none of them had doubted it: mankind's last war was imminent, and the only ones who survived would be his own people, his beloved *phrateres* of thirty lonely centuries.

Lamia had known, as well, that there dwelled deep beneath the surface of the earth, in the fabled Vale of Aphaca which Pythagoras discovered near Indianapolis, the legendary monster,

16

Aether. Immense and virtually deathless, Aether, who guarded the entrance to Antipodes and thus the entry to other dimensions of time and reality, was only appeased and kept captive by the sacrifice of human bodies, people, living or dead, fed to him by her sometimes-lover Vrukalakos.

But she knew now that her brother vampire was torn to bits by Aether and that Pythagoras himself had failed. Surely the valiant band of incredibly ancient Greeks would prove helpless against the greedy Aether. And surely one of us, Lamia concluded at length, should be left alive to prevent that mighty creature from escaping; surely one of the Old Ones should try to halt the final act of human folly which *Logos* predicted: Armageddon. The war that would surely end all wars, since it must end all life.

At last the decision was reached by sheer feminine common sense. While she seemed entirely youthful and altogether beautiful, Lamia was much too old, "too advanced," as she expressed it woman-like, to adjust to death at this point in her life.

After all, Lamia realized with a shudder, there might well be *penalties* for the things she and the others had done in order to sustain life through the centuries. It seemed quite possible that the Almighty, or the gods of Olympus, if her long-dead parents proved correct in their belief, looked askance upon those who utilized the ancient art of *metempsychosis*, or the relocation of one's immortal soul from one body to another body. Unasked. While Lamia was agnostic in her own faith, she'd already tasted a measure of eternity and the idea of spending another three thousand years in the kind of searing flames which Aether tended lacked all appeal.

When the time came that every other ancient Greek paraded through the woods to the Vale and descended into the awesome tunnel beneath it, Lamia invoked her vampire powers to alter her form. She became a menacing female hawk, rising into the night sky above tiny and doomed Thessaly.

She was now on her own, she realized with a shock, for the first time in her life. Always there had been the fatherly Pythagoras to guide her, the security and companionship of an immortal family which shared her dark secrets. It was absurd to feel that way, Lamia knew, but a shiver of apprehension tingled through the tendons of her powerful wings as she soared westward above sleeping Indianapolis. *Time,* she thought, *I need time to consider what to do.* About Aether and the greater monster that was humankind's imminent last war. And about her own unfamiliarity with the ways of the modern world. But time was precisely what she lacked, if the brilliant old leader had been right.

Lamia cocked her feathered head. Not for the

18

first time it occurred to her that Pythagoras, even the genius Empedocles in his writing of the *Logos*, might be in error. In a Greece that was young and gay, only beginning on a course that would make it the intellectual and cultural capitol of the old world, pretty Lamia Zacharius had once been the most brilliant psychic alive. It was that fact which drew the attention of the mathematician-philosopher, to begin with. Her skills as a sensitive were the reasons Vrukalakos, at Pythagoras' orders, vampirized her. In order to keep her alive and use her talents on behalf of the great man's plans for an endless future. She remembered how the more superstitious fools of the period had wanted to sanctify her, to make her a goddess fit to reside on Mount Olympus itself, and how the wise Pythagoras realized she was only a gifted girl-child whom he could employ on his quest for immortality. He had been a father to her until his death at Aether's claws this week.

But the fact remained, however she revered his memory, that Lamia doubted the bombs of annihilation would soon fall. Deep in an eternal blood mingling with that of hundreds of less fortunate beings Lamia sensed that an error had been made.

Oh, they would come. One day, when man and female vampire least expected it, perhaps, this ebon sky through which she passed so silently would be filled with the shriek-and-hiss of long-range missiles. *Going*, she thought wryly, and *coming*. Atomic and hydrogen missiles that made the individual threat of one ancient, anthropomorphic Greek beauty appear puny by comparison.

The powerful hawk's agate eyes squinted against the swirling gloom of night. Ahead, Lamia discerned, rising from the somnolent streets of northeastern Indianapolis, was a black church with its tower piercing the sky. Wings fluttering, she flew into its waiting protection and perched, still in the form of a bird, beside the heavy, dangling bell. Time, she thought again, I must have time. Silence enfolded her in its comforting embrace and Lamia consciously relaxed, sought to release the infinite psychic powers that lurked in the chambers of her penetrating mind. Stillness overcame her. At a glance, should someone have seen her there in the belltower, she might have been some wondrously sculpted gargoyle guarding the churchly music from untimely sounding. Slowly, deliberately, the tentacles of her psychic skills moved outward, ever outward, groping deeper and deeper into the night, across the state, the midwest, to the outer boundaries of her adopted America and beyond, sensitively probing tentacles that touched lightly and bore away dark knowledge without anyone knowing she was present.

Visions, images, pictures filtered back to the

vampire's waiting mind, messages from the U.S.S.R., from China, from Israel, from Lebanon and Pakistan and the Arab Republic. A gathering influx of information from every pressure point in this complex and confusing new world. Lamia shifted nervously on her perch beside the windowless tower and at last opened her hawk's eyes to blink at her present surroundings.

There were tears in the great bird's eyes and she shook her feathered cranium angrily, muttering soundless imprecations from her sharp, rending bill. The fools were going to do it. The plans were laid, not in only one secrecy shrouded segment of this lunatic world, but in many. War would come—but not for at least a year. That, in the last analysis, was the fragment of hope Lamia's psychic probe secured. Devastation was at least twelve months away.

That was the immediate problem thwarting Aether and the destruction he would wreak upon Indianapolis. Lamia nodded wisely to herself. Aether might be slower, his work might take longer; but his presence, too—avid, unsatiated, greedy and endlessly, unreasonably *wanting*—must mean death for all those who encountered him. Her *phrateres* of Thessaly would have had no choice but to leave the tunnel leading to Antipodes open and unguarded. Once Aether tasted living, pulsating human bodies instead of the carrion which Vrukalakos brought him, the

21

monster would only crave more. So it had always been with evil, Lamia knew. It could never be satisfied; quite the contrary, it grew. Like her own psychic sensibilities, Aether's evil appetites groped outward, constantly, in all direction.

How pleasant it would have been to return to young, wise, peaceful Greece; how pleasant if Pythagoras' plans had worked and they had gone *en masse* to an alternate world, a world that wasn't doomed. She did not wish this earth destroyed. In a way, she thought as she swayed on her perch in the tower, she feared more the chaos that would descend upon the planet if Aether's presence were known by all the world's people. Modern humans, unlike those with whom she grew to maturity three thousand years ago, held not the gods of old to their hearts but the image of order. Order, and civilization, and the Pythagorean type of reasoning from which they sometimes grew. It did not please the timeless woman vampire to consider an existence in a world of shouting madness.

The hawk raised its head, straightened its powerful form. Lamia brightened, her wing tips brushing against the bell and causing a shiver of tinkling sound to whisper across the sleeping town below. *One* being—one only—might succeed in halting Aether, in stopping the avaricious monster forever. And might even prevent the outbreak of all-consuming warfare. She nodded sagely. In Lamia's time-sharpened wisdom it was rarely the forces of good that countered evil successfully, but an evil still greater. Good men proved that everywhere, she felt, whenever they went to war and killed their fellow creatures with as fervent and thorough a malice as those unsavory ones who began the war. No, Lamia thought sadly, the gentle judgment of her leader, brilliant Pythagoras, had been doomed from the start. One did not defeat an evil with cleverness, science, or goodness, and one did not escape it by running, either.

*Stopping Aether—stopping the war to end all wars—was the task of someone infinitely more evil and powerful than either of them. It was the charge of the Prince of Fates, the Infernal Power of the ancients, a creature born at the dawning of time, who was himself the* oldest *source of horror and blood-lusting death in history: Demogorgon.*

Satisfied with her choice, Lamia paused and looked down. Heights never dizzied her; it was only depths that troubled the queen of vampires. There had been no motion beneath her of any kind since her strong wings ceased fluttering and her clawing feet enabled her to perch in the bell-tower. Indubitably, she decided, she was alone in this corner of the sleeping city.

Light as drifting feathers, she plummeted to the ground below and hesitated, peering in all directions. She did not wish to be the child, Lythia, again. She preferred being what she was: woman.

23

Lamia looked deep inside, formulated the image carefully, and exerted her dynamic will. The hawk, in hawk form, was gone.

In its place stood a tall, slender, dark-haired woman with incisive black eyes into which a man might cheerfully plunge and lose himself forever. She wore the costume last worn by the girl, Lythia, a simple form-fitting white dress with a deep bodice that accentuated her high, thrusting breasts and perfect hips. The ebony hair reached to and caressed wide shoulders, and framed a face with a sensual mouth composed of a short upper lip and a full, somewhat pouting lower lip. Behind them both, ivory-white and marble-hard, were two jaws of dangerously sharp teeth. The face might have belonged to a woman approaching forty with the total realization that she had never before been quite so truly . . . female.

The door of the church was unlocked and Lamia slipped inside, unseen but wraithlike in the night's long shadows, and glanced briefly down the carpeted path leading to the altar. Her black eyes fixed on the cross only cursorily, then shifted, uneasily but unhastily, to the rows of vacant pews. Lamia chose one at the rear, sat on it with her slender body twisted so that she could look at the open door. With centuries to practice, even a vampire can conquer her little neurotic aversions. She thought again of the man-beast who might save the world, and smiled.

Not that Demogorgon would care in the slightest for the destruction Aether wreaked. There was a long passage of time when merely mentioning the word "Demogorgon" brought instant disease, even hideous death. That, Lamia knew, was not gossip or superstition. She had seen it happen with her own eyes and admired the creature's far-reaching authority.

No, there were other reasons why she believed Demogorgon might honor her request, her plea for help. And, most notably, the fact that he had hungered after her once, with all the puissant power of the god he was, one-thousand years before the Man this church revered. For more than fifteen-hundred years Demogorgon had dwelled in the guise of Baal, the towering being honored by the ancient people of Phoenicia.

Ah, Phoenicia, Lamia sighed, remembering. She recalled meeting Demogorgon, as Baal, in nearby Heliopolis, east of Lebanon on a piece of land stretched lazily along the Mediterranean, and accompanying him to Phoenicia. Even as Baal he had been the most enormous man-thing she'd ever seen with her own eyes, and something lastingly female in her wanted to know him better. She remembered him explaining to her that her people, the Greeks, had named the nation after *phoinike*, the purplish-red hue of fine Tyrian dye which the ancient Semitic Amorites made yet another two thousand years earlier.

25

Demogorgon-called-Baal—*his* people had never dared utter his true name—told her as they strolled the beach how he had used his remarkable scientific aptitude to advance the lot of the early Phoenicians. He spoke with enthusiasm of how they devised the first Phonetic language. And he spoke with cruel amusement of how they yanked the teeth from captured slaves and, inserting them in their own mouths with gold wire, created history's first dentures.

She had looked up his towering, admittedly handsome figure to the noble, ferocious head and wanted him badly, that day. But she also knew the secret of this man whose name she could not utter, a secret that brought him both imponderable loneliness and the reckless malice which people feared. This body, though immense, was temporary. Pythagoras assured her that he was really so massive that no ordinary woman might survive his attentions. Confronted with that fact and yet doomed to powerful lusts that never suffused a man before, Demogorgon had left behind him an entire cemetery of ruined young human women.

Over the next few months in Phoenicia, while he implored her to worship and to love him, the being called Baal achieved miracles that would still astonish the world when Lamia's life took her to distant America late in the twentieth century. This god who craved her so ordered a massive, stone acropolis built in the fabulous city of Baalbek. A citadel with doorways twenty-feet high, to accommodate him when he wished to be himself. Measuring four-hundred feet wide and eight-hundred-and-eighty feet long, this grand acropolis rose more than forty feet above the earth and—Demogorgon told her with almost boyish pride—was constructed of *two million pounds of rock.*

"They shall never know how this structure or others were built," he boasted to her. "They shall wonder about the buildings of Phoenicia to the ends of time."

Lamia smiled, now, in the church pew, as she arose, walked to the door, and peered outside. No one was around, so she walked forthrightly toward the nearest suburban town, quite unafraid of the nighttime she adored. She smiled because she was the only woman alive who knew *how* the giant called Baal built his acropolis—or *why.* None of today's scientists had so much as a guess to make; but Lamia knew.

She knew, as well, that Baal believed man must confess his latent beastiality in harmless ways in order to keep it under general control. It was this reasoning that made his memory cursed by the Christians to come, his reputation twisted and contorted until—by either his own name or by that for which his city was named—he was intentionally confused with Satan.

27

How absurd that was, Lamia thought as she ventured onto the deserted highway and again headed west with the lithe stride of a marathon athlete. Demogorgon—if he really put his mind to it—was *much* worse than Satan! Take, for example, his insistence that the Phoenicians who worshipped him must imbed a corpse in the foundation of each gate of every city. A *fresh* corpse, preferably, although one that was still living would suffice.

On the outskirts of a town named Lawrence, Indiana, Lamia sighed. How was she to locate Demogorgon today? Four centuries after Christ, her courageous Greek compatriot Lacantius, emboldened by man's greatest savior, actually dared mention Demogorgon by name—repeatedly—and sent the vain god-demon into hiding. Into an isolation that existed to this day. Lucan chronicled his going, his pledge to return in triumph one day. Milton and Spenser immortalized his might, and Lamia knew, once, how to locate him in the deep abyss, dwelling with his three sisters in the mountains of Himalaya.

The world might yet depend upon Demogorgon's powers, Lamia felt, heading for an all-night diner near Fort Benjamin Harrison and thinking of the pulsing military throats awaiting her. *If* she could find him, and *if* she could control him. Suddenly impatient to stand beside the behemoth once more and long, impossibly, for him to love her, Lamia willed herself to become a swift, scurrying German shepherd and dashed for the warmth of the diner.

If she did not find Demogorgon, everything would end. Even for psychic female vampires.

. . . The eye of Greece, mother of arts
And eloquence.
                    —John Milton, *Paradise Lost*

I wish I didn't know now
What I didn't know then.
                    —Bob Seeger

## II

It was the particularly indecisive kind of
September for which Indianapolis was noted,
even if the chamber of commerce rarely discussed
it: pregnant with stubborn summerness one day,
rainily dreary and bonechilling the next. Because
Lawrence adhered to the northeast tip of Indianapolis like a forgotten scab, until its excellent
record for services and street conditions periodi-
cally became an itch on the greater Hoosier body,
it was the kind of small, pretty town into which a
person might vanish and never be seen again. But
with its inevitable proximity to Indianapolis, the

two cities reluctantly shared the weather.

Dr. Frank Triladus went to work that morning with a feeling of comfort in his short sleeved shirt and lightweight trousers, then returned to Lawrence with his windows up and his muscular arms freckled with goose pimples. In between, Triladus spent seven hours working at I.U.L.—Indiana University at Lawrence—in concentrated fascination over the archeological artifacts he'd recently acquired.

"They seem to have belonged to the same unknown creature as the other things Professor Calumbo sent along," the teacher of archeology reported excitedly to everyone who'd listen. "I honestly believe we're getting closer to the missing link."

But once he was entering the forty-year old, white frame, two-story in Lawrence and sitting down to dinner with his wife, Mila, Tridalus kept the news to himself. He doubted seriously that Mila would be interested and, as he took the bowl of mashed potatoes from her outstretched hand, he was grateful again that Mila seemed very little interested in anything.

It was a joke so private that he rarely told it to anyone. In Triladus' honest opinion, if Mila'd been intelligent, she'd have been dangerous. The viewpoint was rather less cruel than it sounded on the surface. As he began to chat with her about unimportant matters, he saw again how unani-

31

mated her face remained and how her entire, pretty head seemed dwarfed by her over-all size. Mile was well over six feet tall and had a body to match. Frank knew that she wore a 44-D brassiere and dresses bearing the labeled legend, 20-Long. A lesser man might have considered her grotesquely large and made jokes about the way Russian ladies Olympic teams should *also* take certain tests.

But Triladus had never been an ordinary man, never would be. At a time when the nation's scientific press reported his age as only thirty-two, the I.U.L. professor had already leaped to minor fame due to certain archeological discoveries. Without leaving his comfortable old house in Lawrence, Indiana, Frank Triladus had managed to add tests of his own to customary carbon dating and present fresh theorem about the true origins of humankind.

Moreover, bolstered by hard evidence furnished him by anthropological teammates in Africa, South America, and at various mountain ranges essential to his claims, Triladus began to look like the most likely candidate for answering an ancient question: at what point in prehistory did *homo erectus* and *h. sapiens* break off and *homo sapiens sapiens* begin?

Some four-hundred thousand years ago there were people looking somewhat like ourselves, with brains eighty-three percent the size of ours.

Two-hundred thousand years ago more refined Steinheim man showed up in Germany, giving way eventually to the Neanderthals found in that nation's Neander Valley. Oddly, Triladus knew, the misunderstood Neanderthal seemed to exist in two varieties: large-browed, big-nosed, massively boned ninnies, and a smaller variety not drastically unlike modern man. His kind clung to the earth until some thirty-to-forty thousand years ago when, apparently from the blue, a hunter and gatherer just like us hovered into view. It took them at least another twenty-one thousand years to begin building permanent settlements, and it wasn't mankind's lot to have genuine cities until *circa* 3,000 B.C. Frank knew a great many experts argued that it was longer ago than that, but the question remained: What happened to banish Neanderthal types and produce *h. sapiens sapiens?* What—and *who*—lay in between?

"Where are Livy and Daria?" Triladus asked after a lengthy silence that began to get on his nerves. He referred to her sisters. "Won't they be home for dinner?"

Mila shrugged uninterestedly. "Daria said she would be at the museum until it closed. I forget where Livy said she'd be."

The archeologist frowned but said nothing. He'd tried for more years than he'd care to admit to civilize Livy and doubted that he ever would.

She might at least have phoned. There'd never been a more perverse woman, he felt, than beautiful, blonde Livy.

Despite himself, he opened his mouth and said what he thought. "If Livy'd been male, she would have been a lech. Alistair Crowley revisited. If it's alive and attractive, it turns on Livy's sexual appetite."

Mila arose, a towering figure of a woman, and went after the wine. For a moment Frank feared he had offended her, but then she was back, her colorless eyes dully flickering across his face, still standing as she poured into two tiny glasses. Looking up at her bosom this way, he thought, was like staring at some unclimbable jutting from a mountain side. Still, he continued to admire the soft brown hair she wore cropped close to her skull and the surprisingly fine bone structure of her face.

"It's hard, sometimes," she said slowly, trying to vouchsafe an opinion and finding the words rasping in her throat, "being forever away from the far country. From home." She swallowed and looked at him. "There was a time and a place where people like Livy were understood."

He snatched the glass and downed the wine in a gulp. "We don't discuss home anymore," he said peremptorily, "not any of us. You know as well as I do that there are sound reasons why we can't return to Greece—or anywhere else we've been."

Mila glanced at his powerful shoulders and the way his large hands threatened to crush the small goblet. "I know," she admitted.

"Don't look at me that way," he said, rising to head into the living room. "It isn't all my fault."

"But it's you who wanted to be *here*," Mila's voice trailed after him, husky in his ears. "It's you who's looking. Not us."

What she said was true enough, he supposed, slumping in his easy chair and reaching for the newspaper on the nearby table. But Mila and the other two were women who should genuinely understand custom, time-honored tradition, better than modern women of the United States. They should realize that a man did not mean to be cruel when he decided where his family would go. They should realize that the women accompanied him accordingly, without complaint, with patience and attentiveness to his needs, with absolute support. After all, he could have chosen to leave them *all* behind at the last stop. He, Doctor Frank Triladus, didn't need them because he was the man of the family. *They* needed *him*.

Which made the teacher feel better as he opened the newspaper and spread out the classified pages. He shivered, thinking how chilly it had become again in this damnable midwestern state, and sighed heavily. How much longer would he need to run the want ad and to expend time and energy interviewing people before the right applicant read it and came to his house? *Saboi*, it was wrong to doubt—even for a moment—that he was correct. Triladus knew he was right because it was logical, it made cold geometric *sense*, and a man of science chose no other course.

Sooner or later the right applicant would show up at the front door. He rested the newspaper open to the classifieds on the table and fumbled for his cigar case.

The ad read: WANTED IMMEDIATELY. VERIFIABLE PSYCHIC TO PARTICIPATE IN ARCHEOLOGICAL EXPERIMENTS. EXCELLENT PAY, POSSIBILITY OF EXTENSIVE EXPENSE-PAID TRAVEL. CONFIDENCE GUARANTEED. It listed his name, address, and telephone number.

At the moment he had the enormous cigar going well, with clouds of thick smoke rising above his curly head as he sat back to relax, Frank Triladus heard sounds in the room and looked up cautiously.

It was Mila, immense and statuesque Mila, with something *tiny* clutched in her big hands. The hands were raised to him, demonstrating something, making an announcement. For a moment he couldn't see what it was she held, and squinted.

When he made it out the temperature in the room seemed to rise, sharply. "Great thundering Zeus," he growled, half-choking on cigar smoke. "Are those clothes for an infant?"

Mila's attractive head nodded, batting her eyes at Frank almost coyly. "Yes, Frank, they are. I'm going to have a baby."

If it is unsettling and surrealistic to depart a day of normality and find oneself in the grip of unrelenting nightmare, what must it be like to leave a life that is an unceasing nightmare and stride the earth of mortal man for the first time in thousands of years?

It was an incredibly lengthy journey to the surface of the earth and it had taken Aether, the legendary guardian of Antipodes, the underworld, a long, arduous time. He had been fortified by what seemed to him an endless string of delicious shrieking, living Greeks, many of whom he clutched to his side with some of his great clawed hands in readiness for eventual hunger. But now he had exhausted his supply. The people of Thessaly were no more. And he stumbled through the rocky exit to solid ground, collapsing.

What motivated the immense and ancient, powerful beast to make the tiring journey at all, he could never have said. Although he was the most brilliant as well as the most diabolical of beasts, he remained a beast. To perceive Aether's intelligence, his very special psychological attributes, meant evaluating the deft shrewdness of a soaring falcon, the cunning of a trapped tiger, the mindless ferocity of a mother grizzly bear whose young were slain, the dauntless patience of a house tabby waiting hours for the arrival of a rodent, the stealth of man, and the gluttony of a warthog. But none of that would provide adequate understanding of the creature, because Aether was, above all else, something that people did not understand at all. The infamous beast which earlier humans called a dragon.

Except that in all of time there had never been more than *one* such beast: Aether himself. Utterly sexless in order that nonē of his cruel malice could be diverted, created whole before man could intentionally make fire, the monster might have been an errant mistake of some insidious Satan who sometimes stole the creativity of the Almighty and made such things. But if he was, indeed, the child of evil's primary and immemorial source, the error had been too egregious, for Satan himself, too foul a trick to play on pathetic humankind.

Or perhaps it was that the diabolical creature who devised Aether, who assembled him of countless claws and raging fiery breath and steel-spined wings and tree-tearing tail, privately feared the beast. And trembled in his flaming abode at the Frankensteinian thought that Aether might one day wish for *all* his filthy kingdom, *compete* . . .

The myth of the dragon was recorded first among ancient Sumerians who settled in Mesopotamia five thousand years before Christ. *Zu*, they called Aether then, who stole from the god Enlil all the wise tablets establishing the laws of the universe and ate them. It was Aether, eighteen hundred years before the gentle Jesus, who served the Babylonian queen Tiamet and brought the fires of destruction to man. And it was Aether in Egypt who, called Apophis then, became the mortal foe of the sun god and brought the seas raging aground to drown those who would neither swim nor pray. It amused that part of Aether which remained coldly risible to imagine the confusion his presence wrought when he appeared anywhere and everywhere on earth. Puny people did not know that his subterranean dwelling in Antipodes never limited him to *one* earthy egress. They did not realize that there was a stratum beneath the earth which was forever deviously tunneled, a vast world-encompassing labyrinthe which Aether alone mapped and from which he was capable of rearing his unbearably ugly, long-necked head at hundreds of sites such as Thessaly's Vale of Aphaca.

Consequently, Aether was reported in Babylonia and the nations that became Great Britain and Libya, China and Italy, North Africa and Denmark, Java and France, Holland and the East Indies, Germany and Japan, in British Columbia and Greece. Those humans who ascribed to scientific principles protested, much the way modern thinkers objected to the reality of Unidentified Flying Objects, but were shouted down for precisely the same reasons: too many responsible people saw Aether for him to be wished away.

It pleased the wiser chambers of Aether's complex brain to realize how he became the Christians' symbol of evil and it pleased him more that modern psychology saw him simply as representing man's internal struggle against lust and madness. Like all things that are truly evil, the towering beast knew precisely his own nature and understood that no St. George could ever slay him for good until mortal man accepted the fearful truth.

Perhaps Aether made the difficult journey upward to the peaceful woods of Thessaly because, interwoven in the tapestries of virulence and violence, viable even in the pounding hot heart of sheer malevolence, there whispers an urge for freedom. A hungering, small being who wishes to escape even itself in order to sprawl in the sunshine without torment. From without or within.

In any case, eons ago he'd forgotten what the surface world was like, except for fringing forest. In the past he had ascended only at proscribed half-century levels which were enough to let him forget and, since they began counting Time forward from A.D., he'd never been free to wander. He was fortunate to find himself where he was now, prone on plain earth, yards from remembered trees and brush, allowed to pant and quietly regroup his energies with nothing more alien about than a pointing sign marked INDIANAPOLIS—18 MILES. Aether felt over-stuffed, gaseous, the satiation of his grotesque human meals just starting to wear off. He felt satisfied, basically, as becalmed and lacking in overt desire to maim or kill as his kind ever got.

Slowly, though, Aether raised his massive head and with the taste in his mouth of human flesh and carnage, released a mighty belch. The force of it shot gusts of foul wind cascading toward the trees, splattering against them and bending them, as though a putrescent wind had risen from nothing. A belly that reached nearly one hundred feet in length groaned audibly, the noise lifting like thunder in the quietude of the forest scene.

When his gas had passed, Aether rested his giant head on his front feet with claws many feet long and sighed. The ground trembled. What a fool he had been, waiting all those centuries for the vampire Vrukalakos and the woman bloodsucker Lamia to bring him carrion on which to feed. Why, *living* delicacies were so much finer, so much more filling! He had forgotten that, as with most things, through a tumbling pile of decades that fell away like leaves. Part of it was simply that the living bodies fought back, gave

41

him sport as well as sustenance. They even screamed deliciously when he ripped away an arm or a leg to begin the meal and continued clutching the torso in one idle hand. The eyes he remembered, were especially nice, not particularly filling but olive-like, the way he dimly remembered the small green fruit he had popped into his mouth and crunched years ago in Greece.

Aether lay there on the edge of the woods, blinking his several eyes sleepily, contented by chaos, soothed by satiation, still enamored of evil. It had occurred to him that after he'd rested a few days he would shake off this bloated feeling and see what else he might find among the trees. Not only that, the woods were probably not like the labrynthine tunnels of his home on Antipodes; they were apt to end, and Aether could learn what—and who—waited on the other side.

Before he drifted off, the malefactor remembered there was something Out There called . . . a *world*.

For somewhere in that sacred island dwelt
A nymph, to whom all hoofed Satyrs knelt;
At whose white feet the languid Tritons
    poured
Pearls, while on land they wither'd and
    adored.

                —Keats, *Lamia*

It comes an evil guest . . .
                —Simonides of Ceos

# III

Lamia Zacharius glanced at the scrap of paper in her gloved hand, then back at the two-story house again, making certain she had the correct address. She felt more nervous than she was accustomed to feeling. Only part of it was the structure itself, which gave off strange vibrations of a kind Lamia could not speedily interpret, and the scientist whom the ad indicated would be waiting inside.

She had answered the ad for the simple reason that she meant to lie, if it was possible to do so and get by with it. Wherever in the past Dr. Frank Triladus wanted her to go, psychically, Lamia planned to identify the Himalayas. It was there that Demogorgon was last reported living and, because she could only exist as a bird and fly for limited distances, it was Dr. Triladus whom she meant to take her there.

Lying itself did not pose a problem for a long-lived woman vampire. Lamia was primarily uncertain because she'd never utilized her psychic powers in order to trace events of the past, wasn't sure she really could, and—more importantly— wasn't sure she could deceive an experienced scientist. It was hard to guess what this Triladus would expect of her. Probably, she figured, he would pinpoint some moment of the past and ask her to move mentally across continents and backward in time, to the person or event he had in mind. It could get very complicated, possibly more challenging even than Lamia liked.

While she had used her gifts to probe the present, modern world and learn the terrifying news that World War III was on the verge of beginning a year hence, two different factors were involved. First and foremost, she had traveled thusly only in the present and no one but the Olympian gods themselves could say where Dr. Triladus might wish her to go in bygone years.

44

The second problem also concerned her. Most of her past psychic probes were *generalized*, in the sense that she created a primary focal point deep in her mind and simply willed her unconscious mind to take over. It acquired information of its own selection, not hers, consciously. It might provide anything. But this advertising archeologist probably had someone or someplace in particular in mind and, if she attempted this on any kind of legitimate basis, it would be a new use of her powers.

Increasingly, Lamia thought numbly starting up the lane, she was being troubled by fresh, unguessed and unguessable problems. Although she had long since outgrown any need to sleep in earth from her own Grecian place of birth, she had needs similar to those of any woman alive. One of them was clothing; preceding that, she found, there was a need for money with which to purchase clothing. In Thessaly and the other lands in which she had dwelled with Pythagoras and the rest of the *syndic*, Lamia had left such mundane matters as business up to them. In the tavern near the Army fort where she went after fleeing her fate in Aether's massive caves, she'd been utterly embarrassed by an inability to pay for the wine she ordered. It hadn't even been her beloved *kekeon* wine, but there she'd sat, speechless, with a huge bartender glaring at her.

Happily, good fortune sometimes attends the

insane, the alcoholic, and the vampirized, the less being said about this picaresque preference the better. A burly sergeant from Fort Harrison was kind enough to volunteer payment of Lamia's bar bill. Momentarily, the act of apparent charity saved his life, since she had been noticing the size of his throbbing throat for over an hour. But when, minutes later, the sergeant was pawing at her high, forward-looking breasts and slipping a hairy hand beneath her skirt, Lamia resorted to her own time-tested methods for earning money.

Outside the Sundown Inn bar, cloaked by the obese shadows of a semi-trailer, Lamia had simply torn the soldier's throat out and seized his money. It was her further good fortune that the sergeant was in the bar celebrating his winnings from a poker game and, utilizing the proceeds of lucky full houses and flushes, Lamia was able the next day to acquire any woman's first line of defense: a new wardrobe.

It was hard learning the ground rules, when one was on her own. Not until midday, when sunlight became a problem that no longer killed an experienced vampire but proved as irksome as bright rays on sensitive eyes lacking sunglasses, did it occur to her that she no longer had any place to stay. Going back to Thessaly, with her *phrateres* dead and Aether on the verge of escape, was unthinkable. She was glad, then, when she read the want ad page of the *Indianapolis News* and saw

46

the chance for a world of fresh opportunity.

Splendid in a crisp new suit and spindly high heels, Lamia was physically prepared for the interview. But as she drew near the door, she paused a final time as the first vagrant vibrations she felt returned in force.

It wasn't, she thought, the house itself. It would never be the acropolis or even a nice Greek inn, but the structure itself was fundamentally acceptable. Lamia lifted her lovely head, sniffed. An aroma, she thought, of things gone wrong. She breathed more deeply. Here, she felt, were people who were unquestionably displaced by location, time, position, or unshared interest—or perhaps any combination of them. Lamia trembled. The psychic fragrances she picked up seemed to skew the house itself; the roof might have been out of line an uncanny few inches, the slope of the walls was not quite perpendicular, the whole structure sat at the faintest of uneasy angles to the earth itself.

Lamia took a deep breath and knocked on the door.

"Oh, I've known I had talents other people didn't have since I was just a little girl," she answered him lightly, crossing silken legs. "At first, when one is very youthful, indeed, she believes that everyone can do what she does. But with the passing of time and the gathering of

47

knowledge, a sensitive soon learns how different she is."

"How different are you?" inquired Frank Triladus. He hadn't taken his gaze from her since he let her in the house and Lamia sensed his interest, knew how real it was, and how fundamentally sensual. "I mean, Ms. Zacharius, how far flung are your psychic skills? Have you been clinically evaluated?"

An image of Pythagoras' large, white bearded and maned head came before her eyes. She recalled the kind but thorough way he had examined her, three thousand years ago. "I've been tested by the best but as you may know, not every parapsychological laboratory easily releases its test results." She shrugged her suited shoulders elegantly. "I could give you their names and locations, doctor, but I think you'd find them jealously perserving their own findings."

"I can understand without effort why anyone would want to preserve you or findings about you," Triladus said gallantly.

Lamia gave him a smile and appraised him herself. He was thick in the shoulders and chest, and the thighs as well, but not at all overweight. To a certain type of woman, Frank Triladus might have seemed unusually handsome, largely because of his physique. She was that kind of woman. His massing of black, curly hair seemed almost to perch atop a somewhat angular head with the further contradiction of a noticeably rugged bone structure. His mouth, wide and mobile, contained both a strongly sensual side and a cruel streak, she thought. Triladus was probably close to six-three in height, and he affected heavy woolen sweaters and jeans. Although her plans, here, were entirely businesslike in nature, she found herself responding already to his unique appeal.

In point of fact, Lamia hoped he would try to seduce her. How he would go about it, she wondered from the depths of her inexperience with men at large, she was anxious to learn. "Could you give me some idea of what you would expect from me if I were hired?" she asked in her husky voice.

"Of course." He slid off the stool beside a chrome-edged white lab table and retrieved an object which he held in his two strong hands. "I expect from you the very special clairvoyant skill of a psychometrist?"

Startled, Lamia asked, "A what?"

"A *psychometrist.*" Triladus frowned, began looking disappointed. "A psychometrist is a person who can hold an article from the past and simply by touching it produce information about the owner, his times, and so forth."

"I knew what it was, doctor," Lamia said coolly, lying. "I *am* one. I simply did not understand you."

He raised a brow, encouraged again. Was it possible that she was the right applicant? "I would have thought we'd understand one another quite well. If I'm not mistaken, isn't Zacharius a Greek name, just as my own name, Triladus?"

Lamia smiled. "There are many kinds of Greeks, doctor." Now she was stalling for time. It was perfectly obvious that she would not be asked to reveal information about a person or event from nothing at all. This darling man planned to give her what he had in his hands as a clue. She wondered, idly, if there was the slightest chance that she could really do it, *really* find traces of the past clinging to an ancient artifact and identify them to Triladus' satisfaction. It seemed dubious, doubtful, to say the least. Lamia sighed. "What have you in your hands?"

He turned his body slightly and perched on the edge of his table, eyes averted in thought. "The applicant whom I seek, Ms. Zacharius, will be a participant in something that is at once old and new: *psychic archeology.* I am interested in the origins of mankind—"

"Humankind," Lamia said pointedly, smiling to ease the sting.

"I stand corrected," he muttered. "Humankind. I seek the missing link, not so much a person as a condition and a date and a reason why our species took the monumental leap from a life insignificantly differing from the common ape. A psychic who is gifted in psychometry—'reading' the past by merely handling an object of the period—can be priceless to an open-minded scientist. He—or she"—Triladus interrupted himself to smile at her and simultaneously admire her crossed legs—"can pinpoint the exact location for digs, for example. Describe how people lived at some point of the past."

The woman's heartbeat accelerated. It had occurred to Lamia that whether she could genuinely solve the tests psychically or not, she herself had lived through most of the period that man had been even remotely civilized. Many people and places to whom this charming but rather arrogant archeologist referred could also prove to be directly familiar to her. What's more, Lamia realized, she'd also lived on half the planet earth. With the passing of Pythagoras and the *synod*, she probably had more firsthand knowledge about the past three thousand years than any other living person.

She was eager, suddenly, to touch Triladus' object. She put out her hand. "May I see it?" she asked.

He nodded, smiling slightly, and carefully put into her hands a scrap of soft material, painted a screaming crimson and mounted on a small sliver of wood. There was a rusted, almost black, pointed object stuck through all of it.

Lamia lowered her gaze, cupped the artifact in her hands, and instinctively drew it between her breasts. Triladus' gaze was hot on her, she found it hard to concentrate because of the way he clearly desired her. She uncrossed, recrossed her legs and several somewhat smoky images passed her mind's eye.

*An extremely tall woman, powerfully constructed, naked except for an ill-fitting robe. There was small bleeding from one heavy calf of her leg and Lamia salivated faintly. The woman was in a small room, sitting on something, and—*

"You sought to deceive me?" Lamia cried, half rising in anger to throw the object to the ground in total disgust. "Why, that's nothing more than drugstore cotton painted with Mercurachrome! And—and a needle on which the woman scratched herself!"

"True," he said, watching her, waiting for more. He folded his arms and licked his lips. "So far as it goes."

She stood, still angry. "It's owned by a very tall, strongly-built woman," the vampire said slowly, surprising herself by the way the vision continued even with her eyes open and her concentration broken. "She lives—here, in this old house." Lamia sat again, her nails digging into the arms of the chair. She stared at the cotton and needle on the carpet. "Mila, that's her name! Mila

52

Triladus!" Lamia looked up at him, startled despite herself. "Is she . . . your wife?"

"Capitol!" Triladus exclaimed with appreciation, clapping his big hands. "Right on target and full marks, m'lady!" When he saw her beginning to rise again, he held her there with a gruff laugh and firmly-pressing fingers. "You must try to understand, dear. Many persons have come to my home, imposters or neurotics who could not pass so much as this elementary test. I shall have others worth your mettle and, if you are hired, Ms. Zacharius, you will find that there are many challenges in this house to intrigue your excellent mind."

She flushed, turning away to reconsider. "Minera's brows, I'm just not used to being treated this way." Which was true enough, except that she had just astonished herself with the unknown psychometric talent. At least, she could satisfy the tests with properties of the present. She looked up again. "I think you owe it to me, Doctor Triladus, to tell me now the primary location of your scientific attention. That will, at least, give me some general region of the world on which to focus my skills."

He hesitated before answering. "Perhaps you're right." Then he nodded, his curly hair moving against his temples. "Very well, I'll tell you this much: I believe that we have one primary location in which certain bizarre things happened relevant to the missing ancestors of man. A place quite different from equatorial Africa, the generally accepted birthplace of man." He found and relit his cigar, contemplating her face with interest. "I think we may end up in the Himalayas."

Time is the soul of the world.

—Pythagoras

## IV

"As I may have said before," Frank Triladus resumed, sinking into a sofa and locking his hands around one lifted knee, "psychic archeology is both something rather old and very new. Circles and circles, you know, always returning to where one left off."

"I understand," replied Lamia. She hesitated, not really understanding and, like any good gambler, looking for an edge ahead of the performance. "Before you proceed, Doctor Triladus, would you be offended if I asked for something to drink? My throat seems terribly parched." She paused, wondering about the effect her remark would have. "I walked here, you see."

"Walked!" Triladus laughed as he bounded to his feet. "No one walks these days, no one. Jog, perhaps, but primarily ride or fly."

Lamia joined his amusement, liking this big bear of a man enormously. "I've done a great deal of flying myself. In my more prosperous days. Unfortunately, I—I'm on my own just now and quite low on funds. It was really less expensive to use my legs."

"I commend your choice of transportation heartily then," he answered, his shrewd gaze sweeping wantonly up her silken calves. He scarcely remembered to make the observation a gentlemanly compliment instead of a leering proposal. "I can offer you, among other things, beer or whisky, tea, Pepsi Cola or a good red wine."

Lamia shivered in anticipation. "I always drink," she replied, "a good *red* wine."

While he was out of the room she arose and gave his laboratory a tentative examination. There were a number of experiments and designs, utilizing cards and boxed objects in various stages of exploratory development. She saw something that might have been created from a child's erector set; contraptions with mirrors and dials. Whether he planned to use them on her or not, Lamia could not tell without touching them, as vampires historically had a sound appreciation of property rights. It was always the Appolonian village tyrants who came to burn the castle down. Lamia stooped to peer closer. There were—judging by names printed in Triladus' handwriting—subliminal perception tests, some variants of the Rorschach, specific feedback, psychological and physiological variable tests, and some others involving spiritual and engineering constructs. Most of them were unfamiliar to the tall and lovely woman, but they no longer especially concerned her. She had proven, in one swift psychic flood, her own capabilities—to her own satisfaction, if not Frank's.

When he returned with a silver tray, a chilled bottled and two chilled glasses, she permitted her fingertips to graze his knuckles as she accepted a glass and the feeling was electric. Lamia wondered if he'd felt it too.

"Where was I?" he asked, taking his seat. But he watched her studiedly as she raised the glass to her full lips and sipped. "Ah, yes. Historically, psychic archeology can be traced at least to Frederick Bligh Bond in 1907, a bespectacled and gentle architect intrigued by the ancient Abbey of Glastonbury. The abbey was a lost citadel and Bond wanted to excavate it. Glastonbury, of course, is a celebrated place in England, Miss Zacharius—reputedly the home of King Arthur where Joseph of Arimathea brought the blood of Jesus—and Christianity—to Britain. These legends had already fascinated much of the world by the beginning of this century, but no one knew many details stretching back before the eighth century. That was when King Ine of Wessex

57

erected the first portion of the abbey. Three hundred years later it was ravaged by fire but was soon rebuilt. In point of fact, it became a sort of western Vatican until 1539 when the jealous Protestant regime went so far as to order even the stones to be carried off. Needless to add, my dear, the treasures there vanished first." He smiled wisely at Lamia. "Enter, in 1907, the extraordinary Mr. Bond, a 53-year-old member of the prestigious Somerset Archeological and Historical Society who already had a passion for the abbey's history. In time, Frederick Bligh Bond would be called a madman with some twenty-four distinct personalities. Or, according to Bond's biographer William Kenawell, one who 'ranked among the truly great minds of the day.'"

"It sounds like a mystery story," remarked Lamia, who'd lived through more than a few herself. "Do go on, please."

"Well, it's too complex to tell in full. But the facts are that after using the skills of a psychic friend to acquire automatic drawings of the buried abbey and himself becoming director of excavations, Frederick became far more fascinating than *James* Bond ever dreamed of being." He paused to see if Lamia understood that he meant, by "automatic drawings," sketches conveyed to the unconscious mind without the subject realizing that he was drawing at all. "Bond, you see, believed in the somewhat occult theory of Gematria, a theory that ancient buildings' actual measurements conceal secret codes revealing the builders' knowledge. Soon Bond was personally getting 'messages' from long-deceased monks who offered information about the abbey—information that was generally correct or not, to this day, proven *incorrect*. He was in touch with something called the Company of Avalon, the Watchers from the Other Side."

Lamia sipped her wine and washed it between her teeth. "Fascinating. How long ago did this Company live?"

He paused. "One message, in a hand distinctly *not* that of Bond, ended—in Latin—'I am Johannes, who speaks from memory of the matter. The time of which I spoke would be 1492, as I remember it.'" Triladus swallowed the rest of his wine in a gulp. "The proof, as they say, is in the pudding. Strange as it sounds, Frederick Bligh Bond was able to find and reconstruct a surprising number of buildings which alerted modern man to their intriguing existence. And he did it with the aid of more than two dozen people who were *dead for more than five hundred years*—monks, stewarts, clockmakers and cowherds, artists and builders described in massive detail! Some said Bond could literally have written twenty-five or more biographies of long-dead people who lived in the fifteenth century!"

"Mr. Bond was the first, then?" Lamia remarked over the lip of her glass.

"Probably not the first, but the stimulus to others. Other psychics through the years have delved, from the depth of their trances, into the past, of course. But probably the most interesting after Bond," Frank Triladus restlessly got to his feet and began to pace the room, "was Stefan Ossowiecki, who provided a positively *massive* amount of information in *saboi*—all one could wish! About a Magdalenian culture which thrived in Europe more than fifteen thousand years ago!"

For the first time in a while Lamia frowned with private concern. Fifteen thousand years was distant, indeed; it was twelve thousand years before *she* was born! If this delicious Greek doctor expected her to plunge so deeply into the past, she would have to do so on the strength of her ability as a psychic, not on guesswork.

Triladus turned up the thermostat on the wall and rubbed his hands together against the autumn chill. "It was at the beginning of the Scorpio period in 1941 when that famed Polish psychic was tested by a Dr. Poniatowski from the University of Warsaw. Ossowiecki, the son of a chemist, a man with the gift of psychokinesis— moving objects by the force of his thoughts— proceeded to submit to a vast series of hour-long testings and provided priceless archeological information from Paleolithic prehistory to Acheulian times when man first made stone axes.

During this rather raggedly-conducted period the Wizard of Poland described not only artifacts and important events in the lives of people dead for tens of thousands of years, but described *them*, their emotions, their religions and fears. As was true of you, Miss Zacharius—"

"Please call me Lamia," she interposed.

"Gladly. As in your case, Lamia, Ossowiecki utilized psychometry, a psychic skill of clairvoyance described first in 1842 by Ohio's Dr. J. Rhodes Buchanan. If Ossowiecki was only guessing, his imagination was phenomenal. He was never confused by objects given him to hold without a clue as to their carbon-dated period of time. He returned immediately, visually, to just the correct moment and location. Some of the things he saw concerning the Magdalian culture have been verified since his examinations. Subterranean huts with large stones used for chairs— he was correct about their dimensions—and the hunting of reindeer with bone-tipped spears. Just as Ossowiecki said in 1941, about a people *never seen by modern man*, their skulls proved to have large noses and deep set eyes. They proved to be small in height as he predicted, to have had large hips, and they sewed leather for clothing with fine-eyed needles made of bone—just as he indicated years before! The Pole claimed they were buried after cremation, which did not seem to reach that far back at all. But he again proves out.

Now we know cremation was done twenty-five thousand years ago, in Australia."

Lamia leaned forward to fetch the wine bottle and poured a finger more into her glass. "You said that there are also contemporary proofs of psychic archeology, I believe."

"Yes, there are. It's been of use in Canada, Mexico, Tennessee, Arizona and the Soviet Union. Jeffrey Goodman did a good book on the subject in 1977, after his own experiments at Flagstaff. More recently, the Marea experiment took place in Egypt where psychics George McMullen and Hella Hammond did some remarkable things. They correctly located ancient Byzantine sites with sub-floors made of smallish, round marble tiles. McMullen had given their size and it was only off five-eighths of an inch. The wonder of it, as Stephen A. Scwartz reported, was that he had located an object the size of a quarter out of terrain measuring two hundred twenty-five square miles!"

"Well, doctor, it sounds like you expect a good deal of me," Lamia murmured.

"More than you may suspect," he said cryptically, ignoring her lifted eyebrows and rummaging on the table for a moment. He handed her something. "I won't insult you with trickery this time, Lamia. Take your time, please, and tell me what you can about that."

The room fell utterly silent except for the

steady *tink*, *tink* of autumn rain on the roof of the old house. Frank Triladus knew that it was difficult for any psychic to perform on cue, that their best work tended to be done spontaneously. He was experienced enough as well to know that sudden uprisings of emotion—strong emotion— were devastatingly destructive to any psychometrist attempting a reading. And so the unseen clouds of quiet descended round their heads and shoulders, and Lamia's handsome, dreaming face for a while was the only clear reality in the world. Time passed, but Doctor Triladus waited patiently.

The object in Lamia Zacharius' firm hand was possibly ten to twelve inches in length, made of a sturdy wood and painted black. Clearly, it was neither new nor ancient and she wondered at its importance. *Steady*, she told herself; *logical thinking won't ever do this job.* Her eyes closed and she hummed quietly, melodically, her fingers working at the wooden piece while her hands shifted back and forth, up and down. Her features twisted in an ecstasy of internal effort. "Someone—evil—owned this," she said finally in gentle tones, not looking at her host but opening her eyes to stare at the fireplace. As if responding to her, the glow of the flames crimsoned her forehead and cheeks. She began to perspire. "It was owned by someone who was indisputably the possessor of a dark and evil soul. A German, I think, and he is dead. Mercifully, for human

63

people." Her eyelids batted. "The period of time would be . . . this century, yes, the late thirties or the early forties."

With self-control Triladus kept from nodding. His job as observer, he knew, was neither to endorse nor criticize or get in the way. His task was to let the psychic speak her piece, wholly, say everything she had on her mind. Lamia's central challenge came now, however; he was sure of that. Once, several weeks ago, a squat, homely man who was basically sensitive had gone this far successfully. But then his logical, conscious mind obstructed him. He shifted his focus to the practical left hemisphere of his brain and blurted out the name: Adolf Hitler.

And he was wrong.

"Now I see," said Lamia softly, her own deep-throated woman's voice a counterpoint to the tinkling rain striking the old roof, "a hideous private castle. It is owned by this dreadful man, or stolen from some aged baron whom he dispossessed. A great banquet hall comes into my view. Around the sumptuous table in that vast hall are thirteen chairs, and"—Lamia's fine nostrils wrinkled and she made a disapproving face—"and it is a ghastly parody of the Last Supper. As well, twelve of the chairs serve to represent the twelve signs of the zodiac. The owner believes that if he has men from all twelve signs he represents the world and enhances his terrible power. The thirteenth chair, of course, belongs to this living monster." She held the wooden piece out to him gingerly, by the tip. "This object that I hold, Doctor Triladus. It's part of a leg from his chair, a souvenir of our victorious forces. Correct?"

Now the archeologist nodded, clearly impressed. He leaned his husky body forward on the sofa, refraining from comment but hoping she would get the rest of it right.

Lamia's luminous eyes fixed hypnotically on his face. "A pagan cult existed—was practiced— in this man's castle, something vaguely Satanic. And worse. He killed little homosexual dancers for amusement. Sometimes, when his own men were under an adverse planetary influence, he had them destroyed as though to pacify the heavens themselves." She swallowed. "The man was the head of Hitler's feared SS forces and his name was Heinrich Himmler."

She did not wait for him to validate her statements. She threw the broken black chair leg to the floor in obvious distaste and wiped her long fingers on the side of her skirt.

"Admirable, my dear," Triladus exploded. He beamed on her, then scratched the crown of his tightly-curled black head and smoothed the hair into place. "I believe you've passed all the tests that I require. If you'll accept the position, I'd like you to work with me."

"Doctor, I am no innocent. I want to be fair

with you and I've seen some dreadful things during my life. A few men have called me an angel but it may well be that I'm something rather less than that." She managed a laugh. "A death angel, perhaps. Sometimes those near me have died." She looked up at him from lowered lids. "You, I believe, are made of stronger stuff. And I will work with you only if I do not have to deal with such filth as that damned chair leg. Whatever else I may be, I'm no defender of the Nazis."

"It was merely a test," he replied.

"What in the world, Frank," came a voice from the door leading to the private quarters of the house, "have you been accusing this girl of?"

Lamia turned and saw tall, muscular Mila Triladus and two other women entering the room. Instinctively, she shivered.

Left to herself, the serpant now began
To change; her elfin blood in madness ran,
Her mouth foam'd and the grass, there-
    with besprent,
Wither'd at dew so sweet and virulent . . .
                              —Keats, *Lamia*


Sin is strong and fleet of foot, outrunning
    everything.

                              —Homer



## V



Despite her usual unruffled and evaluative
outlook, Lamia was surprised when she saw the
titanic size of Mila Triladus, who had already
begun wearing maternity clothes. Customarily,
large women did not show a pregnancy as much as
smaller ones but Mila seemed determined to be an
exception. Such weight as she'd put on only added
to her image of hugeness and the petite features of
her small, pretty face struck the vampire as

incongruous. There was, as well, something vapid and inconsequential about the Triladus woman which Lamia sensed was *purposely* projected. The first glance told her that Mila might be no great shakes as a conversationalist, but that she was as shrewd as a fox.

Yet she offered Lamia a warm, fleshy smile as well as her hand and Lamia rose quickly to accept them. She winced as the big woman's stubby fingers fastened on hers, the squeeze of a healthy Greek wrestler, careless with his power. It was hard to judge how much of the clasp's hurtful strength was intentional.

"Just as we were passing the door," Mila began in explanation, "we heard our Frank hiring you. Of course, we were all eager to see what you were like." She held on to Lamia's hand but turned her head to the archeologist with disarming candor. "I honestly didn't know you had such good taste, Frank. Ordinarily you don't hire people for reasons that might have to do with their beauty or sex appeal."

Triladus smiled, shrugged, and puffed deeply on his cigar. "That's Mila's way of paying you a sincere compliment, Lamia," he said slowly. "I think. One can't always be certain."

"Oh, it is!" Mila trilled. She did not seem to realize that Lamia was returning the handshake with all her own considerable strength. "You're absolutely lovely! I'm so glad Frank will have

68

another pretty face to look at now, considering how gross I'm getting with my pregnancy."

Lamia retrieved her hand and tried to sort out the many things she was hearing. "Thank you for the praise, Mrs. Triladus. It's always nice to hear from another woman."

"Mila, call me Mila, because we're all going to be great friends." Finally she remembered her entourage and stepped back, revealing them. It was as if they had been eclipsed by Mila's great size or even just materialized there. "Lamia Zacharius, these are my sisters. Daria and Livy."

"Hello," said Daria, softly, putting out a hand in a manner that approached shyness. She looked at Livy out of the corner of her eye, as if to ask if this were acceptable. Daria was a tiny brunette with a nice figure, no more than five foot in height, her liquid brown eyes expressive but hesitant and her full lips inclined to purse. While Lamia estimated her age at twenty-nine or thirty, Daria affected a costume that might have come from the Junior Miss department; a frilly white blouse and gaily-hued full skirt. Not that she wasn't pretty, Lamia thought, because she was in a rather timid, cute way that she'd never cared for. Lamia's immediate judgment was that Daria seemed dominated by her sisters.

The third sister, Livy, extended her arm and Lamia wondered, for an instant, if her hand was about to suffer further damage.

Instead, Livy's touch was at once extremely gentle and strangely sensual, lingering against the palm as if its owner was reluctant to break the contact. Younger than either Daria or Mila, she was slightly shorter than Lamia but athletically trim and slender. She had a sweeping torrent of pale, blonde hair that reached the small of her trim back and the bluest two eyes Lamia could recall. There was, in fact, something disconcerting about those eyes. They seemed to stare, watchfully, appraisingly, even when they weren't directly focussed on Lamia's face.

Perhaps she wears contact lenses, the lovely vampire mused. Or perhaps she has lesbian interests. The unsettling azure gaze was more direct and penetrating than that of Frank Triladus and, if it did not precisely hunger, it certainly quested—and questioned. "Frank does his best to make even his home and laboratory a man's world, my dear," she said, speaking in the voice of a network news announcer, cultivated and precise. "But we've been known to liven things up. I hope you're the lively sort?"

Lamia thought about her three thousand years of life and smiled a private smile. "I can still get around pretty well, Livy. But I'm new in Indianapolis and Lawrence, and anxious to get settled in somewhere. Do any of you know about a clean, inexpensive rooming house which might take in another boarder?"

"I suppose I'd be prying," Doctor Triladus put in, "to ask where you come from and why you've decided to stay here?"

"Yes, I'm not anxious to go into all the details." Lamia spoke gently, to avoid sounding rude. "Things became . . . unpleasant, where I was. It seemed to be best to make a new start."

Livy lifted her chin challengingly. "Then you aren't married, is that right?"

"No," Lamia replied. "I'm foot loose and fancy free."

"I'll just bet you are," the blonde replied, her grin both aggressive and suggestive. She turned to Triladus. "Well, brother-in-law, we have a mystery woman on our hands."

"Mila," said Daria, her quiet tones striking, drawing attention, "I have an idea. We have another bedroom on the third floor, one that isn't being used. What would you think of letting Lamia take it until she can put down roots more permanently?"

Mila blinked, confounded by the idea. Then she found her smile. "That's an excellent idea, Daria. We're a very casual, easy-going family, Ms. Zacharius, and I think you'd like it here. Is it all right with you, Frank?"

"I don't see why not," he agreed at once, pouring the rest of the wine into Lamia's glass. "It isn't being used for anything and, if Lamia's on the premises, I can take advantage of her psychometric flashes whenever she has them."

"I wouldn't want to put you out in any fashion nor would I mean for this to become a permanent arrangement," Lamia said swiftly. When she looked from one face to another, her sensitive brain shrieked a warning. It wasn't an impression of hostility, that wasn't quite it. It was more the feeling of a freak posed naked on a carnival platform, gawked at by geeks—or perhaps it was the feeling of a mouse trapped in a cage. In all her long, Pythagoras-protected existence Lamia had never been in this kind of position before and didn't really know what she should say. "Honestly, Doctor Triladus, if I stay I'd want you to subtract my rent from the salary you pay me. That's the only way I could consider staying here."

"Well, that's no problem, Lamia. I'm certain we can work things out amicably all around." He finished his wine and made several wet, thoughtful rings on the slick lab table with the bottom of his glass. He looked up again, flushed, running a hand nervously through his crop of jet hair. It had seemed that he might have something to add, a warning, perhaps. Instead, he smiled. "There now, it's settled. We're glad to help."

"It will be nice having you," Mila remarked. Her tone wasn't dubious or doubtful, but whispered to Lamia, eerily, of enjoyment she would derive which could not now be voiced.

72

Livy arched one colorless brow and moved to stand beside Lamia. Prepared to show her to her room, the slender woman's body pressed against Lamia slightly, almost with an air of ownership. "It certainly will be. Nice. It should make matters all the more . . . lively." Then she took their guest by the elbow, her hand proprietorially cupped round it, and looked deeply into Lamia's dark eyes—questing, perhaps, or questioning. "Why it will be like there are four sisters in this gloomy old house instead of only three." She led Lamia to the door where Triladus stopped them.

"Shall we start bright and early tomorrow morning?" he asked, his smile flickering nervously. It occurred to Lamia that he was reluctant to let her go with Livy.

She nodded to him and went out the door with the blonde. Two steps into the interior of the house and she was freshly surprised. Lamia had entered through the front door and been taken down a short, neat hallway to Doctor Triladus' immaculate laboratory. Here, however, she was shocked by the dismal, unkempt appearance of the house. Didn't Mila or her sisters do any housework? Patches of flooring showed through the faded carpet and here and there she saw spidery cracks in the walls fairly screaming for re-plastering. Above her and Livy, at the top of the steps, the lightbulb had burned out. Wriggling shadows played on the red-carpeted landing.

73

She felt the blonde's blue eyes watching her every move, Livy's pliant young body pressed close on the narrow rise. Any doubt about Livy's sexuality left Lamia; proximity with her own hot-blooded body had Livy panting sharply.

*What am I getting myself into?* she wondered, confused by the sharp turns in her life. *How far will I have to go along with these people in order to locate Demogorgon and stop Aether?*

"Here's your room," Livy whispered in her ear.

Our scientific efforts to make things right
sometimes seem like rearranging the deck
chairs on the Titanic.
                    —W. Norman MacFarlane

Leave Hell's secrets half unchanted
    To the maniac dreamers.
                    —Shelley, *Prometheus Unbound*

# VI

It had been Lamia Zacharius' preference, for
absolute ages, to be up early in the mornings.
Whenever she could, she enjoyed being the only
creature of stealthy motion, a shadow-like image
of dogged substance drifting ghost-like through a
sleeping house. After all, if she arose early enough
it was still dark. It gave her the comforting sense
of familiarity she'd acquired through centuries of
wakefulness in the period of the ebon nights.
Vampires, in the truest of senses, are creatures of
habit, defenders—in their way—of the status

quo. Not one of them ever existed who liked new homes, who minded the monotony of silent corridors, intriguing half-closed doors or glimpses of the helpless sleepers within.

In common with most of her kind, as well, this beautiful woman once found it necessary to avoid the rays of the sun. It was true, however, only through the early segments of her existence on earth, before she began to rise above the simple neuroses of her species and get some of the control over herself that she always enjoyed over others. There'd never been any truth to the superstitious notion that she would rapidly deteriorate, fall to sullen ashes in sunlight. There never had been.

But during her girlhood of approximately five hundred years Lamia found that sunshine not only gave her headaches and eyestrain but disturbed her menstrual cycle. It was quite bad enough, in Lamia's view, that she was the one woman who suffered through periods for over a thousand years without adding to it with migraines and red-rimmed eyes. Gradually, then, as she approached true maturity and the brilliance of womanhood that would be hers for the remainder of eternity, Lamia experimented with Yoga and certain Chinese incantations in order to conquer her problems. It took time, but that, with beauty and lethal killing prowess, were what she had more of than anything else. Eventually she reached the point where being up in the daylight did little more than make her vaguely apprehensive. Since she was able to translate that to clever wariness, she'd succeeded in turning a disadvantage into an advantage.

This first morning in the Triladus household, then, she was dressed and moving through the unlit halls before anyone else. Outside the archeologist's room she paused, seeing the door ajar, and peeked inside.

Doctor Triladus was sprawled on his back beside Mila, one sturdy arm draped across her burgeoning abdomen, his lips parted as a horrendous snoring sound filled the room. Lamia stared at him and, seeing the man was both naked and inordinately well-built, found an old hunger crowding in on her. Like the other vapid superstitions begun by ignorant villagers everywhere in the world, there was no truth to the notion that vampires could only have oral sex. It was simply that they were "born"—or, putting it more accurately if offensively, "born again"—perpetually hungry or thirsty.

That element of her kind's existence also troubled Lamia, and had for decades. It was just one more coffin nail in their reputation which she considered unjustly acquired. She'd even planned to do an article on the topic for some broad-minded magazine one day.

It was charitable when vampires drained the

blood from human beings because, after all, the predators *were* able to handle solids very nicely and oft times preferred to tear out the throat for a truly satisfying meal. But whether the human was left maimed or vampirized, she felt it was ordinary consideration to leave the throat relatively unmarked unless she was absolutely famished. Nobody, dead or alive, liked to walk around with an ugly hole in their neck.

For a few moments more she stared at the naked man and noticed, with fascination, that he was becoming aroused. Why that should be, sleeping next to the gross Mila, Lamia had no idea. When she reached the point that she was on the verge of leaping across the floor to the bed, however, she used a self-discipline taught her by the ages, closed the door behind her, and turned into the hallway with a hiss. Someday, perhaps, doctor, she told herself.

Several yards down the corridor Lamia paused again. This door was closed but her senses informed her, reliably, that the room was occupied—not by one sleeping sister, but by two. An image of Livy beside her on the stairs last night rose sharply before her mind's eye and, in simple prurient curiosity, Lamia opened the door.

They slept like two tight spoons, Livy and Daria, each of them perfectly nude and perfectly lovely. Lamia had been a sexually aroused person for only several hundred years and had never experimented with intra-sexual relationships. Yet something ancient and deeply felt, rooted inside her like the soul of selectionless sexuality itself, could not but admire their beauty. The blonde Livy faced Lamia, her breasts almost pendulous with small pink nipples. The way her long legs were tucked into a fetal position, only a fringe of yellow pubic hair was visible below the waist. Behind her, petite Daria's dark hair rained in beauty on her pillow, lips pressed against Livy's neck in sleep. Her breasts were the kind that flattened out and the nipples were generous of proportion, brown as her pubic hair.

Did Lamia draw the obvious conclusion that the sisters thought incest was best, or was something subtler involved, like the timidity Daria felt and a concommitant need for her strong sister's comfort? Shrugging, she turned to leave, then saw something startling on the floor beside the sleeping young women. The faded carpeting had been torn back, brutally pulled off the wood, and there, scribbled on the floor in white and scarlet chalk, was the first pentagram Lamia had seen in years. Did this mean they were witches? Was the whole Triladus clan, she wondered, a vital part of a coven?

Certainly it was a peculiar household, the vampire mused with mild disgust. Closing the door softly, she felt a shiver of something close to fear trickling along her spine. The sun was coming up now and it was going to be a nice, warm, autumn day. Already sunlight spilled through the kitchen window, unfiltered by the open curtains, giving the double-sink an unhealthy, glistening look of life. Even the nearby sideboards seemed to wear that glowing skin of living things and, with a shudder of distaste, Lamia drew the curtains and turned away.

She adored doing this, always had. Prowling like a burglar through the possessions of somebody else. She wouldn't steal a thing, of course. No vampire stole anything but blood and life. But it had been so long since she lived in the same way ordinary people did that she found it engrossing to poke and prod and lift their objects. It was as if, eventually, she might find lying beneath a frozen package of french fries or a half-gallon carton of two-percent milk another container stamped, "Normality. Taken twice a day it restores God-given life used up in the hurly-burly of routine. Take only as prescribed."

In the refrigerator Lamia was surprised to find largely butcher-wrapped white packages of meat. Curious, experimental, she pulled back the tape and looked at several of them: steak, lovely slices of porterhouse and T-bone steaks. Finding a bottle of tomato juice, as well, she withdrew it, poured a glass and walked over to the upright General Electric freezer. The door was almost frozen shut, but she tugged on it, hard, and it opened, making her take a step backward.

Again, crammed full of excellent cuts of meat. Well, Frank Triladus was no vegetarian, that was certain. No stranger to the delights of biting into thick, resistive flesh herself, Lamia found herself admiring the archeologist even more. She started to close the freezer door, then saw a package on which someone had scribbled the word "liver." Lamia paused, then took it out and unwrapped it. She toted her tall glass of bright-red tomato juice—she'd added no ice—and the uncooked liver down the corridor to the laboratory, licking at the frozen meat as if it were a popsicle.

It hadn't been possible the day before, to examine the place closely. She'd been much too busy answering the doctor's questions and passing his little tests. Now she took her time, beginning with the books filling four shelves on two of the four walls.

There were many volumes on archeology, others on history and prehistory. She saw massive textbooks and handsome coffee table books on long-lost civilizations and, as she flipped through them, the remarkable procession of humankind's ape men paraded from the Pleistocine before her watchful eyes. Not surprisingly, too, she encountered a number of books telling the long, luminous history of Greece, pausing quite naturally to read what one of them had to say about Pythagoras. The modern schools of thought seemed split about her brilliant, late mentor. Some claimed he was not only a mathematician, philosopher, and teacher, but a metaphysician—a man who knew more than any other of his time about these talents which would one day be termed "the paranormal." Others insisted that he was a pedestrian thinker who ramrodded others into accepting his philosophies and somehow limited the flow of free thought for several hundred years.

Lamia used her preternaturally sharp teeth to take a bite of the liver, then placed the remnant on a table as tears crept into her eyes. Sighing, she returned the book to its place on the shelf. She knew a man could be many things, that he was almost unlimited—within the boundaries of his God-given intelligence—in what he could achieve. Until that moment when he too narrowly defined himself as "good" or "bad." Pythagoras was a moral man in his way but insisted that lasting morality derived from proper use of the mind and talents and not vice versa. He himself had told her his view: if a man was right, and to his knowledge *knew* that his stand was clearly right, it no longer was a case of throttling other viewpoints but of *preventing* ideas that were inherently wrong from being circulated. There could not be two rights; however close they might seem to be, a person had to decide which was more precisely true and cling to the correct one forever. "Truth is too precious," Pythagoras said once when they were circling him in rapt attention, "to be shared with that which lies, even if the lies are more intriguing."

"I see you're enjoying my books."

Startled, Lamia popped the last bite of frozen liver between her lips, chewed twice energetically, and swallowed. "Good morning, Doctor Triladus," she said when she could. "I—couldn't sleep."

"The place seems strange to you, I imagine," he said, sinking into his seat at a desk and sipping from a coffee cup. He looked rested, dynamic and youthful to her. He'd shaven his obviously heavy, black beard and donned a suit beneath his white lab coat. "Or did Livy bother you?"

Lamia started. To cover her surprise, she slowly took a chair opposite him at the desk and made herself finish her tomato juice. "No one in your family disturbed me." She wanted to leave it at that but couldn't control her curiosity. "Why did you ask—about Livy?"

He frowned. "To tell the truth, Livy has a good many bizarre notions about sexuality. I'm not certain she has anything or anybody at which she'd stop." He gestured with his hands, dismissing the problem as his responsibility. "In her own way, she's good hearted enough, I suppose. But I don't expect my employees to be subjected to sexual escapades not of their own manufacture. If she causes you any trouble, Lamia, be sure to notify me."

"I will," she promised, meaning it. "I will." The awkward conversation slowed and she raised her arms to indicate the hundreds of volumes in his shelves. "You have a fine library, doctor. A reader could spend many profitable hours here."

For a moment he didn't answer. She realized that he was staring closely at her, his eyes dark with hunger. Then he looked away with some embarrassment. "My interests," he replied steadily, "are catholic. Anything that is from deep in the past—interwoven in complexity with periods of time we cannot know—intrigues me immensely."

"Anything?" Lamia repeated softly.

"Anything," he nodded firmly. "There isn't enough time in a day to look into everything that whets my appetite. To me, my dear, the past is a book that was written in invisible ink. A very good, interesting book. What I shall expect of you is psychic assistance in locating a means of bringing the ink back to visibility."

She hesitated. "Would you like to know what once happened here, in this room?"

He was surprised, and laughed. "Well, I had in mind a more distant past than that, Lamia. But tell me, please."

"I have touched the walls, the floors, and they are the way they have been for decades." Her eyes locked with his as she spoke, held them hypnotically. He didn't fight it. "This house was built originally for a couple who moved in and spent their honeymoon here. This room," she smiled faintly, "was their bedroom."

Triladus smiled back. "I see. Go on."

"They were very much in love, this rich boy and the poor girl he loved." Lamia put out her arm to touch the nearest wall with her fingers, almost caressing it. "He was red haired with freckles, an adorable young man. She was Irish, auburn haired with sassy blue eyes and hips that rustled from side to side when she walked." Subtly, a change came over Lamia's face. The smile vanished and her eyes widened. "But there was . . . trouble. Terrible trouble; a burglary." She frowned, angry at the past, at people she had never known. "The boy was obliged to watch as the burglars assaulted his bride. Raped her." Now she found a lump in her throat, tears in her eyes. "When it was done, when the evil men were gone, the worst happened. The boy killed the girl with his own hands, then shot himself." Slowly, Lamia lifted her hand and pointed to the corner of the room to Frank Triladus' right. "There, over there."

He looked where she pointed and shuddered. "I didn't know of them," he said, rapt with attention. "You're an extraordinary woman, Lamia, not only because you can see into the past." The corners of his mouth turned up as he appraised her. "You have a deeply self-involved side. I can see that you look after number one, as we all tend to do. But you care, don't you? You *care* what happens to people, and how?"

Lamia didn't reply for a moment. Instead, she listened to the house breathing to itself, mumbling old secrets like a man getting on in years, anxious to be heard a final time. "I care about some kinds of people," she said softly, at last. "Some people are here to be hurt, I think. That's my theory, at least. Some are created to become victims; they ask for it their entire lives. Others, though, are dear. Others aren't *meant* to be wounded and, when they are, nature gnashes its teeth and terrible things transpire." She leaned forward over the desk to rest a palm on his hairy wrist. "Others, like you and me, fall in different categories. We're aggressors, I believe. The kind the world must suffer, like it or not. Because aggressors get things done."

"What have I hired in you," Triladus whispered, "beauteous Lamia? A psychic and psychometrist, a friend and aide—or something *more* than that? Perhaps a dark conscience to remind me of those things I try to forget?"

"Time always tells," she said simply, slowly sitting back. "One must be patient until it speaks."

He took a breath. "I didn't tell you the entire

truth. About my expectations for you and psychic archeology." He rose, glancing briefly at her, going to the window. Outside the temperature was warming the way it had been earlier in the month, and sunlight turned his cheeks the yellow-orange of fallen leaves. "It is true that I seek a missing link, a period of time and an explanation for pre-historic man's mighty vault to a creature much like ourselves. I want to know how that happened, and why. But there's more. There's more."

"Please, doctor," she said, again fascinated with him. "Tell me."

"Only if you'll call me Frank," he inhaled. "Well, Lamia, I search for my *own* roots—the impossibly long line of my own ancestry. There, by the cabinet against the wall, you will see a small trunk." He watched her nod. "Here is the key to it. I have been paying considerable money to a Professor Calumbo for his investigation through-out the world—considerable money. What he has assembled, in that trunk, is a series of priceless—and in some cases, no doubt, valueless—artifacts which his team claims to represent the whole line of my family's past. Do you remember that I told you I expected much of you?"

"I remember, Frank," she said.

"It is enough, I imagine, to keep us working together for evermore." He inclined his head, suggesting the trunk. "You'll find in there objects from all over the world. The Triladus line, while primarily Greek, roamed. Explored, adventured, impregnated ladies all over the world. Apparently we did so forever. Now, something happened right before Jesus, in the region of the Himalayas. Calumbo thinks we'll have to go there, investigate certain digs he's personally set up. Because there's too much fragile stuff to send." He took her hand. "Lamia, I want you to use psychometry on *every* old artifact in that trunk, tell me what you see about my family. Do it at your own pace, anywhere in the house. We'll record every step because another goal I have is validating psychic archeology for good." He looked away, mildly embarrassed. "Truth is, the Triladus line, under all its different names, seems to go . . . *all* the way back. You will find us in prehistory, I'm told. Calumbo says it is even money that my own ancestors were a part of that mysterious link we've been looking for so long."

"You ask a great deal," she said soberly, challenged. Her eyes glowed. Again Triladus had mentioned traveling to the Himalayas where she might locate Demogorgon.

"It's a tall order, I know," he said, coming to her and, standing above her, taking her hands. "But it is one I think you, of all people, can handle. Because of people like you, lovely lady, it's possible that what we say is 'lost to antiquity' isn't really lost at all. Just . . . temporarily misplaced."

"I appreciate the opportunity."

When she said it, Lamia half-closed her eyes, believing that he meant to kiss her.

But he only compromised by stooping to press his lips fleetingly against her forehead. When she remembered the way he'd looked in bed, lying aroused on his back, she longed to reach out to him and pull his body against her.

Instead, during the afternoon, she took the trunk of ancient artifacts up to her room and began attempting once more to attune herself with those things that she grasped. To her annoyance, however, she found herself distracted by the unfamiliar appearance of the room, longing for her house with Vrukalakos back in Thessaly. What a monster he had been, in two literal interpretations of the word; but he had known her needs—understood them—and at those rare times when he shared her desire, the vampire had fulfilled her totally.

Dinner was another matter of listening to Mila's strangely off-center complexities, Frank's nodding agreement with the remarks around him, Daria's timid and sporadic offerings and Livy's double messages. Lamia was happy to retire to her room shortly after eight o'clock.

It was already dark in tiny Lawrence and Lamia began to feel more herself. For comfort, she stripped off the dress she'd worn during the day and, clad only in bra and panties, stood at the window peering down at the silent black streets. She focused generally on Doctor Triladus' hand-carved chest and swirling mists rose like dust below her, clouding—then illuminating—her inner sight.

This time something came through but it wasn't what Lamia had expected.

Only once had she caught a glimpse of Aether, the creature from Antipodes—the heaving, hot heart of the world—and that was almost two thousand years ago, in Persia. No one who ever lived could forget the monstrous thing once they saw him, but memory has a way of dimming with the passing of years and now, as he materialized clearly as a sharp and reliable vision, Lamia hugged her arms around her breasts and tried to blink him away.

He would not go. He was out of the tunnel to hell, aground, edging his way into the woods of Thessaly. *Enormous,* she thought, *the damned thing is enormous.* She shuddered as she saw his great, plaited tail swinging from side to side, cutting into trees with the force of a thousand woodsmen's axes. Some of them snapped in two and fell like matchsticks.

She saw, ahead of Aether in the woods, a small boy who had roamed away from a vacationing camper. He couldn't have been over six years old and he was lost. Immediately Lamia's heart went out to him. She even considered running to the window, willing herself to become a winged creature and fly to him, lead him back to his worried parents. But then the vision cut to Aether once more and she saw, with heartrending certainty, how close the dragon was to the boy. She knew she could not possibly get there in time, knew that her powers were not so great as Aether's in any case. She'd heard how Aether literally ripped Vrukalakos to bits and realized with horror that each of them was damned to remain alive—sentient—to the end of time. Many times she had awakened, crying for the stupid, evil thing, seeing the way his legless feet padded aimlessly, painfully through the woods, the way his armless hands groped pointlessly— the way his bodiless head hungered, with doomed eyes beseeching an end to their torment and agony. She did not dare confront Aether herself; she could not. That must be the task of Demogorgon, if she ever located him.

The pain of responsibility which she could divulge to no other being filled her heart with despair. Momentarily she cursed Pythagoras, and Vrukalakos too for giving her this terrible "blessing" of immortality—an immortality which sometimes meant the horrid killing of pathetic men whom she could never know. Alone in her room, lonely and afraid, Lamia Zacharius began to cry.

But when she awakened restlessly kicking back

the covers in the middle of the night, her mood had shifted, unasked. She was again the fiercely determined creature she'd always had to be, a woman who allowed nothing to stand in her way. Filled with desire she knew she would *have* to have Doctor Frank Triladus, that she would *have* to make love to him with every magically sensuous trick she had acquired over the bloody centuries.

And if Mila got in the way, Lamia concluded grimly, why, Mila would simply have to die.

Or what more subtle, foul, or savage
  fiends
People the abyss, and leave them to their
  task.
                    —Shelley, *Prometheus Unbound*


# *VII*


For several days Lamia virtually lived either in her room or Triladus' laboratory, delving into his enigmatic treasure chest of ancient secrets. She would grasp an item—a tool, article of clothing, manuscript written in a lost language, scrap of furniture—and harmonize her .thoughts and feelings with it until she was able to see her visions clearly.

Dutifully, sometimes with Frank present and most of the time alone, for she worked better without the company of others, she spoke her findings into a tape recorder with which he had provided her. Because the artifacts were simply laid carefully in the chest, unlabeled and in no order whatever, she might spend one morning with her unconscious mind in the fifth century, the afternoon one thousand years before Christ, the next morning in the days of the American revolution. She knew that Doctor Triladus kept a huge book locked away in a safe with drawings of the objects scrawled on each page so that he could verify her findings against the small collection of data he'd been sent by Professor Calumbo. Sometimes it irritated her to realize that he might at least be able to tell her if she should look to Italy, or Switzerland, or the Americas for the part of the past she sought. But most of the time she realized and accepted the fact that by conducting a series of blind experiments, with no clues at all to assist her, he was fulfilling his intention to validate psychic archeology.

There were several connecting threads Lamia had already discovered, and some of them were extremely disconcerting.

First and foremost, she had been able by mid-October to whisper into the tape recorder her psychic certainty that Triladus' Professor Calumbo was right. All the artifacts belonged to the same family. In the midst of any "far travel" Lamia did anywhere, she was always aware of something she called "personal furriness." Pressed by Frank Triladus for a further explanation, she tried hard to put it into words.

"It is only rarely that I actually walk among the

people of the past, rarer still that they see me," she said recently. "Obviously, I do not dare be an actual participant at such moments or I could alter the flow of history. I seldom even feel that I am literally present, only watching. What I usually encounter is a sequence of quickly-flashing scenes, like those comedy blackouts on TV. A brief, very fast glimpse of persons or places, sometimes with sound. Sometimes, too, there is a far-off thumping I'm aware of—a frightening, underground sort of sound which I almost believe is the noise of the earth's heart beating. But most of the time there's a terrible, agonizing silence that I don't care for at all. The impression, I suppose, that a ghost has of utter isolation, of not-beingness or not belonging. As if I'd flowed back in time on its rippling underside, a roller coaster aspect of a time that seems to be . . . *fraying*, coming apart. That frightens me too. The idea that I may be doing damage to—to that which holds us all together." She'd hesitated, trying to finish in a way that he would perceive. "Whenever I've been in far travel, everybody I encounter that way gives off something *different* than what today's kids call 'vibes.' It isn't anything that strong or real. It's . . . a *furriness* emitted by each person of the past, and everyone has his own distinctive kind." She'd shrugged helplessly at him. "I suppose it's the aura I sense; but instead of seeing it, I find myself sort of hearing and smelling it. Like walking into a furriers and just knowing how pleasant it would be to rub your hands over all those beautiful furs."

"That may be a very apt description," Triladus told her. "Because like the people of the past, the furs were once alive, too."

The secondary feeling Lamia had when she was testing the artifacts in the chest was similarly off putting and hard to describe to the archeologist. Once, when he had been away at Badler University all day teaching his classes, Lamia confronted this level of truth and considered leaving the old house in Lawrence. She wasn't sure she could tell him what she felt.

But there was nowhere else to go now, and when the rain was drizzling down out of angry skies that seemed to slobber with open-mouthed fury, and the thunder seemed directly overhead and rumblingly pregnant, Lamia spoke her latest discovery into the microphone of the tape recorder: "That personal furriness I mentioned before, doctor. I've come to associate it with something dreadful. You see, since I picked up that first old piece of pottery and held it against my breast, I've seen repeated scenes of tragic death. Of deaths that are caused, of people who are made to die—hideously. I'm never quite able to see the culprit or what he or she is doing to make them pass away." Here she paused, groping for the right words. But there was no light or carefree way to put it and at last she plunged. "The thing is, whenever I see people collapsing of strokes that are intentionally caused, or falling off cliffs, or falsely accused and hanging by the neck until they're dead, I feel that personal furriness I mentioned, and it *belongs to your family. To the Triladus clan.*"

Although weeks later she finally got her nerve up to ask him his reactions to the information, Lamia was surprised to see his apparent lack of interest. He made it clear, by softly changing the subject, that he did not wish to discuss the matter at all. And Lamia decided that Triladus simply felt shame for the things his family had done through the centuries and, having neither a way to justify their wrath or any personal responsibility for the things that happened, he saw no point in probing for the rest of the truth. It was obvious that he was content merely to listen to her reports, taped or personally offered, and jot down the information she furnished him.

Relationships with the other women in the house proved to be as difficult as Lamia had imagined they would be. Obsessed with the child she carried, Mila Triladus scarcely spoke a word to anyone most of the time, satisfied to rock her days away and occasionally weigh herself. If she went to a physician, Lamia wasn't aware of it.

She had the impression that Daria would like to

have been friends, but everytime they fell into tentative conversation, Livy put in an appearance and instantly tried to monopolize the conversation. Since the pretty, slender blonde seemed to have no interests except the various aspects of sexuality, conversation with her quickly palled on Lamia. It wasn't that she was a prude. She simply didn't want to talk about her own experiences and was rarely aroused by people who harped on their own. Interestingly, however, Livy eventually discussed her preferences openly. While she might well have spent the night before in the bed of a man in Indianapolis, she was just as quick to describe the thrills she found in the arms of women she knew. In an uncomfortable way, Lamia admired her candor.

But she was uncomfortable about it mostly because she was sure, absolutely sure, that Livy was as determined to bed her as she was adamant about winning Frank's attentions. Happily, the blonde with brilliant blue eyes rarely touched her and refrained from openly demanding that they go to her room.

What puzzled Lamia most, as chilly autumn crisped its way toward colder winter, was Doctor Triladus himself. A woman knows when a man responds to her beauty, her personal appeal, and there was never a time when curly-haired Frank failed to look hungrily, even avariciously, at her. But that was as far as he went and Lamia had no idea why. She only awaited his call.

It was possible, of course, she mused, that despite Mila's size and ever-increasing grossness (she'd begun to let herself go, often humping her way through the house reeking of stale perspiration) the archeologist adored her. It sounded unlikely, but men had ways that were entirely bizarre, in Lamia's estimation. There was no telling how a given individual male might feel about anything. Perhaps he was nostalgic for a younger, trimmer Mila.

But on the occasions when Mila grumped, or sobbed, or lost her valkyrie temper fully and shouted at him, Frank either urged her to close her mouth or turned from her—whipped away—with an expression on his olive face of the greatest disgust Lamia ever saw. Once, when she asked him if he loved Mila, he replied with surprise: "Of course, I love her. We have been together for an infinity, it seems. But in the sense that you mean it, Lamia, I've never cared for her at all." He paused and made a face. "She has all the sex appeal of an eighty-year old sperm whale."

Perhaps, Lamia began frantically to strive for the reason, it was that Frank Triladus was a privately religious man. Maybe the concept of adultery itself went against his conscience, or he was simply afraid of the consequences.

But now she felt she'd always remember what he said when, getting up her nerve, she asked him about his religious affiliation: "My dear Lamia, I am the one man you know who has every reason to believe in a great Force that created us all. My faith is unshakable. Because of it, I would never attend a church or bow my head in prayer. It is quite enough to bear the snickering insults of One who would make a man such as I without foolishly asking for His later attentions."

*A man such as I.* She pushed the words around in her head, knowing they were angry sounds, the sounds of a person who was outraged, even infuriated by what he'd been asked to endure. But what, other than towering, Olympian-sized Mila, Lamia could not imagine.

On the evening of the day that Frank swore to his peculiar faith, turning away from her with feverishly resentful eyes when she tried to comfort him and learn why he felt that way, Lamia retired early and rested on her solitary bed. She meant, eventually, to arise and fondle some of the objects from the chest. By now she had acquired the habit of carrying her tape recorder everywhere, never knowing when a vision from Triladus' past would come to the forefront of her mind. Sometimes she felt that she was losing her own reality in the present, fading away little by little until she found her real feet bathed by the waters of the Aegean, or the Nile.

Indeed, Lamia at times would like to have peered into a mirror to make sure that her flesh remained solid and beautiful. But try as hard as she could, it has never been possible to rise above the vampire's curse of the mirror. Something innate in her species, some neurotic curse laying deep inside her, cancer-like, wouldn't allow her to peer directly into a mirror. Once, many decades ago, she'd wanted to learn if it was true that she threw no reflection and walked within feet of a vanity mirror owned by her friend Dolly Madison. But even as her fingers closed round the handle, she'd dropped and smashed it, too nervous to hold on. "Seven years' bad luck," Dolly told her cheerfully, and Lamia nodded, thinking, more like seven thousand.

The expression "vanity mirror" gave Lamia a deeper insight into her problem. Mirrors were unquestionably invented for women who wished to track the course of their threatening beauty, when young, and its decline as they aged. Mirrors were the typical female's means to the art of makeup, that ancient deception practiced not by creatures of the darkness.

She knew that Yorkshire women believed that if they broke their mirrors they would lose their friends, and wondered about the special vanity of English ladies. Of course, they were always a canny, collected race. Two hundred years ago— Lamia half giggled when she remembered seeing it practiced—several British acquantances of hers had helped a mirror breaker by sweeping up all the pieces and splinters, casting them into a fast-running stream to shake away their misfortune. Before that period, elsewhere in Europe, people covered their mirrors with cloth when someone died in order to avoid a similar fate. Lamia knew that one was true because she'd torn the throat from an overbearing, tax-collecting burgher master to see for herself.

Many times, of course, Lamia had wanted to see if her hair was in place, her lipstick straight, and did not dare find out. To her that meant that gazing into a mirror remained a vain gesture. Vampires, born not of man and woman but reborn by other means, dragged away from the lip of the destroying grave in the old nick of time, enjoyed the good fortune of staying, always, the same. New hairstyles didn't help, not really; even with the contemporary clothing Lamia looked the way beautiful young Greek women looked, three thousand years ago. She remained the same, dreary, boring year in and dreary, boring century out. Lamia stared at a wall blank except for the incongruity of a Norman Rockwell print showing a young girl getting ready for her first date.

It was probably a blessing, though, she figured. Not to be disturbed by changing styles. They trapped a woman, kept her from using her time and her mind on important matters. Matters such as those she had to look into this very night. Because, to Lamia's chagrin, she knew that this

102

was her time of the year.

Lamia had succeeded in either eliminating or delaying most of the traditions incumbent upon her as a vampire. Unlike those who had been more recently exposed to the complex and gruesome ritual of vampirization, she no longer found any difficulty in eating most foods. She adored all kinds of meat. Angelfood cake no longer made her pause a moment, because that was only nomenclature and the way it added inches to the waist was distinctly *not* angelic. Whatever she wished to eat or drink posed no problems for Lamia anymore and hadn't for hundreds of years.

Once she had found it necessary to keep a scrupulous calendar with weekly dates, circled in bright red pencil. She didn't get pregnant if she failed to venture out but she did get evening sickness, and grouchy. Even bitchy. But while she no longer had to attack the helpless regularly, Lamia was still under the physiological and psychological obligation of making periodic forays into the night—of being obliged to make the boring decision of whether to rip away a jugular or vampirize someone she scarcely knew. Always something of an elitist, Lamia generally settled for death or maiming.

Physiologically, she knew, it was a question of suffering iron-poor blood and dangerously low blood pressure if she refused to attack. It gave her the serious risk of passing out somewhere and

103

being given a physical examination—something she did not dare allow happen, ever. She remembered her friend Pasteur telling her once that the lowliest intern would know, instantly, that she survived by extraordinary means. Early in the current century she'd taken a lot of vitamins with iron, and $B_{12}$ shots, to no avail. Psychologically she'd found that failure to snap an occasional throat left her uneasy, uncertain about her own potency as a vampire. Doubts of that kind permeated every aspect of her life. Back in Thessaly she'd found herself quibbling with Pythagoras over the quality of her living quarters and once accused him of showing Vrukalakos partiality because he was a male vampire. Really, at times like this, she had little recourse except to satisfy her personal needs. And in an enlightened age of women's liberation, Lamia felt, who could blame her?

She became a soaring raven whose blackness blended against the Indianapolis night sky and, after a few hesitant passes above the Triladus two-story, decided to fly southwest. Before, living with Pythagoras as a father figure and Vrukalakos as a cunning advisor, she'd had the route to desirable targets marked out for her. Patient as only family men could be at such times, they'd told her gently what to do and where, careful not to say anything cross that would upset her. She longed for them now but it was to no avail. She'd have to score on her own.

Gradually, the city of Indianapolis changed from hundreds of acres of pleasant middleclass homes to a growing business community. Modern office buildings rose from nowhere to confuse her, making her realize that her choice of a raven was a hasty one. These structures were too high to fly over and, as she identified a street sign as North Meridian, she realized that the combination of office and highrise apartment buildings posed serious problems and risks. Colliding with one of them could not kill her but would damage her transient, feathered body and send it plummeting to the pavement. The idea of being swept-up by some garbageman humming Golden Oldies by the Supremes had little appeal for her. Worse, someone from a zoo might collect her while she was stunned and she could come to her senses behind cage bars.

Finally, after passing an enormous insurance building and then being obliged to flap all the way around an old hotel, Lamia dropped to the ground beside a servant's entrance and became herself again. A wino, propped against the side of the building, looked at the bottle of cheap sherry in his hand, back at Lamia, and threw the bottle in the garbage can.

She began strolling, aware that as she walked the lights of neighboring buildings were getting brighter. To her right was a package liquor store and, beside it, an adult bookstore called "Grapple's." On down the block she saw the mended red canopy of a nightclub and gathering crowds of people. Surely she would find the man, the victim she sought, here. Already there were vehicles slowing down, honking their horns in the friendliest of ways.

To Lamia's pleasant surprise, most of the people standing idly on the corner were women. One or two men were there who seemed to know all the girls and rushed from one to the other, apparently urging them to stand up straight. How nice, she thought, to see a truly integrated group out for a good time! Why, there were white and black women speaking briskly and openly together, some gesturing broadly and putting back heads full of glittering white teeth to express their hilarity. It was true that they might be somewhat overdressed for the occasion, a few gowns being overly-vivid of hue and others slashed to the waist. She even doubted that any of them wore underclothes at all, judging from certain telltale bulges Lamia's sharp eyes made out.

But how badly she wished she could become a friend of theirs, be accepted as easily as they seemed to be. Why, even as she formulated the thought an expensive black car with low license numbers pulled up to the curb, one of the women rushed to open its door, and she was inside the vehicle in a flash! Without anything more than a few roughly whispered words in which Lamia caught the expression "around the world." Surely it wasn't possible for the elderly gentleman in the automobile and the young lady he'd just met to be planning a cruise so quickly! If it *was* possible, well, she would need to change her point of attack to this prime location (Lamia scribbled a note, slipping it into her purse) between sixteen hundred and twenty-five hundred on North Meridian street. In any case, it was certainly the gayest, most bustling and enthusiastic place she'd seen since leaving Thessaly.

"Psst." Lamia turned her head at the noise, saw nothing. "Pssssst!" She looked again and found the source of the sound.

Parked several car lengths back from this boarded-up drugstore in front of which the interracial party was going on perched a nine-year-old Volkswagen. A man inside had his head poked halfway through the window and was making the peculiar noises, apparently to her. Lamia pointed her index finger between her breasts, questioningly, and the man in the tiny car gestured wildly with his hands. She went over to see what he wanted.

"How much, sweet thing?" he asked.

Lamia hesitated. "How much for what, sir?" she inquired.

"C'mon, c'mon, I ain't got all night. Don't get coy on me." He was a middle-aged, overweight man wearing glasses and there was a lot of perspiration drenching his face and collar. "How much for—for what you do?"

It was Lamia's turn to be surprised. How could he possibly know? "I've never charged for it before in my life," she said frankly. Because the door was open and the night was getting chilly, she sat on his car seat and looked deep into his eyes. "What I do is absolutely free."

"You tryin' t'tell me you're a virgin?" asked the middle-aged man, frowning incredulously. "Ya gotta be twenty-five or older. Older, I think."

"I haven't been a virgin in three thousand years," Lamia said truthfully, puzzled. Why was this fat fellow volunteering?

"Don't get smart, goddam it!" He looked in his rearview mirror carefully, then at the other women on the sidewalk who were watching them. "If ya wanna do some business, tell me yer price, okay?"

Lamia brightened, understanding. "Your soul," she said, simply, curious enough now to touch his heavy throat with her fingers. "If you want it sucked vampire style."

"Jeeeesus, lady, yer too much for *me!*" He took another look at her, regretful at losing his chance of utilizing her lovely body, and shoved her out of the car. Gunning the motor, never knowing how fortunate he was, he peeled away from the curb muttering, "Free whores! Thirty-year-old virgins!

Throat sucking, f'Chrissakes!"

Dusting herself off, Lamia felt the grip on her forearm before she caught the whiff of expensive male cologne. The fingers hurt but, when she tried lightly to pull away, they only tightened.

It was a youthful black man wearing a three-piece suit and a ferocious glare. "I know you?" he demanded, his voice a rising basso. "You one of my ladies?"

"Let go of my arm," Lamia said coldly, twisting.

"I doan think so and that means you're in even worse hot water, baby doll." He began dragging her down the sidewalk and then into the darkness of an alley. "I seen nerve before, real balls, but you got to take the cake! The en-tire cake!"

Lamia shook her head, trying to understand what the man was saying. By now they were several yards from North Meridian Street and he still hadn't released her arm. "I do not have to take any kind of cake," she said coldly, "I do not have any real or artificial balls, I am not your lady, and you are to let go of my arm at once!"

"Shee-et fire!" he exclaimed, his heavy brows meeting above his squat nose. "You got to be taught some manners and I mean right now!"

The well-dressed man began yanking her arm behind her back, the acute pressure bringing an instant bolt of pain traveling the distance from her elbow to her throat. His cologne was powerful against her cheek. "Mebbe when you got some Emily Post drilled into you, girl, somethin' *else* goin' be drilled inta you too!"

When Lamia resisted, more put out than she'd been in years, the distance traveled by the pimp was the measurement between life and eventual death. Too quickly even for him to cry out, he was flying several feet through the shadowed air and caromming off the nearest wall. His hands clawed the air, his eyes rolled. Lamia was on him in an instant, one knee driving all the breath from his vested stomach. Her hands locked swiftly around his head, one below the jawline and the other beneath the rear of his skull. His eyes bored into hers with dawning realization, awful terror.

Lamia made no effort to twist the head all the way around because that wasted time and energy. Instead, she lifted *up—straight up—*as sharply and as strongly as her considerable power permitted.

The ligaments and tendons in the pimp's throat stood out like cords of rope and then, along the full length of each of them, tiny pinholes of blood popped out at the same moment the vertebrae at the top of his spine snapped like so many buttons torn from an old shirt.

Lamia leaned over the man who had just died two inches taller than he was in life, her scarlet tongue licking away the fine dewdrops of blood that polka-dotted the ligaments of his ruined throat. Then, as lightly and easily as a little girl playing with a doll, she threw his entire body in a different direction so that she could watch the mouth of the alley over the top of his head.

Long white canine teeth fastened in the dead pimp's left jugular, bit, and then met. She swiveled her own head, just a little. Lamia had no intention of turning such a cruel man into a vampire and couldn't, now that his soul had escaped, even if she wanted to. Her only plan was to sate her appetite and this foul-tempered, well-dressed creature was nothing more to her than a sort of psychological tampon. As blood spurted fountain-like from the ripped jugular and she lapped it up, ever tidy and fastidious. Lamia paused to blink. Why, as the throat began to drain, had she pictured in her mind's eye the image of Mila Triladus' blonde sister, Livy, beckoning her from a bed?

. . . Ere eve's star appeared
His phantasy was lost, where reason fades,
In the calm'd twilight of Platonic shades.
*Lamia* beheld him coming, near, more
    near—
                  —Keats, *Lamia*


Black it stood as night,
Fierce as ten furies, terrible as hell,
And shook a dreadful dart . . . *Satan* was
    *now at hand.*
           —Milton, *Paradise Lost*


# VIII


The infant in Mila Triladus' swollen belly wasn't the only thing about the Amazon that was growing.

Her temper seemed to enlarge almost daily, just as her control of it lessened—dangerously. Lamia carefully avoided Mila at all times. That wasn't extremely difficult to do since, even under the calmest of normal conditions, Mila's pounding footsteps were ringing. Heavy, authoritative. Now it was often possible to hear her coming two rooms away and whenever she did Lamia did her level best to be safely out the door before Mila arrived.

She certainly wasn't afraid of Mila, that wasn't it. Angered or calm, Lamia Zacharius possessed an eternal strength greater than that of any living and normal man or woman. What she had done to the pimp in the alley wasn't exceptional, in her point of view. But in her old-fashioned, traditional viewpoint this house in which she resided belonged to Lamia's hostess as much as it did to Frank, and she didn't wish to be asked to depart.

That was especially true after what had happened on North Meridian Street. To her ancient Puritan heart, Lamia remained shocked and, by now she'd had an opportunity to figure things out. It was obvious to her, at last, that the other gaily-bedecked women gathered on the corner were prostitutes and the man whose jugular she'd bitten was a procurer. The very realization of that gave Lamia a bad taste in the mouth which she combatted with several bottles of mouthwash.

The last time she'd seen prostitution at work was in a fine house in Troy, owned by a Greek aristocrat named Oad. That was thirty centuries before, but she had never forgotten the painted beauty and overt sexuality of the whores Oad kept on the premises for his delight and that of his rowdy male friends. Since he was a tight-fisted man, the aristocrat even charged his wine-guzzling companions for the ladies' services and took half the money for himself, saving it in a large vase. Once when Lamia's mentor Pythagoras dropped by unexpectedly, the parsimonious Greek was so startled that he sat upon the vase to conceal it. Lamia smiled remembering the great mathematician's rare sense of humor. When John Keats wrote his famous poem, old Pythagoras delighted in telling any of his *phrateres* who would listen that he'd already seen Oad on a Grecian urn. Laughing jovially, he'd added, "If Oad had saved his money in a bag, I could report that I was eye witness to the sack of Troy!"

Having witnessed ladies of loose virtue blatantly hawking their wares on a public street corner was a genuine affront to Lamia's sense of the proprieties. What she had done in the alley was only a matter of life and death, in her opinion. Besides, the victim was clearly a worthless specimen who, like Oad, survived on the immoral labors of his ladies. While she reluctantly confessed a neurotic fascination for their occupation, Lamia also swore to herself that she never wanted to see such an ugly site again.

Several days afterward, when they were eating dinner late because Frank had been delayed at the university, Lamia learned that other changes were taking place in her hostess. Quite without warning, Mila looked up from her virtually untouched plate to address them all. "This afternoon I was searching for a book on Frank's laboratory shelves. Pregnant women get . . . uneasy . . . about their children and I wanted something scientific about having babies." She tapped the table nervously with her blunt fingers. "It was chilly so I started a fire in the fireplace."

"Yes?" Triladus prompted her. "What happened then?"

"The first thing," said the towering mother-to-be, biting her lower lip, "was that the f-fire caught hold at once. Without artificial help. That implies—unexpected visitors."

Daria, anxious to be helpful, brushed back a lock of dark-brown hair and spoke up. "The baby, perhaps. Since we don't know what it will be, it's unexpected." She blinked and finished lamely, "Sort of."

"But then the fire drew badly, Daria." Mila gripped her sister's wrist. "You know what that means, don't you? It means there's evil at work in this house."

"Come, come, I think we're all a little advanced for such superstition." Triladus sounded weary and a little put-upon. "Why, Mila, you haven't gone out of your way to look for omens in years. Really, my dear, you're much healthier without

115

trying to—to read some covert meaning into everything."

Lamia was fascinated by this new side of her hostess but said nothing. She had her own problems, a feeling of sleepiness that made it hard to concentrate. Stifling a yawn, she sensed that Mila wasn't yet through with her revelations.

"Frank, I haven't told you about the cinders." She said it in a breath. "Frank, they f-formed *coffins*. Almost all of them."

"Oh for God's sake, Mila, grow up," snapped Livy, reaching for the bowl of carrots. "Are you just talking about the shape of the cinders? The way we did when we were little girls? Don't you know that's just an old-fashioned game?"

Mila nodded. When thunder cracked like a gunshot over the top of the house she winced and glanced in fright at the ceiling. Tinkling, the chandelier trembled but held. "They always l-look like either cradles or coffins, Livy. You remember that. And all the cinders formed coffins, even though cradles would have only meant my b-baby." She swallowed hard. "Death in our house is imminent. We might as well face it."

"I'll clear the grate of embers before I go to bed," Triladus said softly. He'd put his fork down and was staring at Mila, hard-eyed but obviously concerned for her mental health. "If I remember the myth, doing that will chase away the ill for-

116

tune. All right?"

"But that still isn't everything that happened." The enormous woman's hand, surprisingly small and pale, began twitching and she had to rest her soup spoon at the side of her plate. "Later, you see, I was resting. I—felt bad, Frank, I really didn't feel good at all. That's when Livy came to the door." Lamia blinked away her sudden sleepiness and saw Mila turn her tiny head to stare, almost accusingly, at her blonde sister. "Livy knocked three times. Frank, she did it: one time, two times, three times. Just like that. Deliberately."

"Oh, damn," Daria whispered. "Greek families of old always believed that it meant death if one was sick in bed and heard three knocks at the door." She glanced with fright at Livy, who made a small laughing sound and shrugged it off. "It *did* mean that, Livy, you *know* it did!"

Before the blonde lesbian could answer there was a shattering bolt of lightning that flashed by the window like a dagger plunging into the earth. Immediately the dog next door began barking frantically, then put its head back to howl. The lights blinked twice, threatening to go out, and Lamia half-rose from her chair in alarm.

Now Mila was quiet with morbid confidence. "Did you hear that?" She cocked her head and rested her hands in her lap. "The lightning, the dog reacting to it. They're omens of some kind."

117

She lifted her head to peer at the others, one by one. When she spoke her voice was tense with terror. "The only question left is: which one of us will it be? Which one?"

"Stop it! That's enough of this claptrap." Triladus fumbled in his pocket for a cigar and found it. "You're only upsetting yourself, Mila, and that's no good." He paused, then fastened his gaze on her for a ploy. "Don't you remember the other superstition? The one saying that a woman who loses control of her emotions risks marking the child?"

"I'm serious, Frank, I truly am." Mila shook her head, refusing to listen. "I want you to honor our old customs if it's m-me who's going. Please promise me you will obey them if anything happens. Make sure my grave is dug east to west with my head to the west." She paused. "I must be able to *see* what happens . . . if I'm called someday. And be sure to bury me on the south side of the church, for—

"Next thing, Mila," sneered Livy, "you're going to remember that the baby might be born on Christmas. According to the old ways, he'll be able to see ghosts if that happens. And if he has a caul over his face, he'll be able to see the future too."

Mila ignored her completely. "Just promise me, Frank. Please."

He caught the sincerity and fear in her expres-

118

sion and slowly, seriously nodded. He flicked a cigar ash. "If it will make you happier, my dear, I promise to do all those things."

Lamia roused herself from the sleepy feeling to touch Mila's sturdy arm. "Nothing is going to happen. I'm sure it isn't. Everything will be fine."

Surprisingly, Mila looked her straight in the eye and said two sentences before rising to rush from the room. "Don't take everything away from me, Lamia. Don't take my b-beliefs too."

Alone in her room, Lamia was too sleepy to finger the artifacts in the trunk, and when she had undressed felt so exhausted that she didn't bother slipping into a nightgown. Naked, she collapsed on her bed and soon fell sound asleep.

Dreams invaded her helpless mind, tumbling torrential falls of impossible images and dimly-sensed apprehensions. Ordinarily Lamia never dreamed in color, but the nightmares befalling her then were incredibly vivid. Coiling colors that ranged from garish greens and riotous reds to delicate weeping tinges of yellow and grave grays, abruptly interspersed with flaring intense white balls of sheer, glaring light. Sometimes there would be a face formed from the cascading kaleidoscope: Vrukalakos, his fangs bared; Frank Triladus lying naked on his back; the maternal Mary Graham from Thessaly with tears streaming down her cheeks; wise, old Pythagoras, his lips moving but unable to communicate sound. Each time the face was swiftly lost in tinctures of swirling crimsons and blushing blues, borne off—silently screaming—into an abyss where, her unconscious mind believed, mighty Aether lurked behind the *next* prismatic slice, gaunt and hungry. She became dimly aware that she, herself, was falling, falling in the way that nightmares suspend time and gravity, drifting feather-like toward the maw of Antipodes. *Jaws,* enormous *jaws* opened wide, flecks of saliva flying. There were rows of teeth like swords, a belch of scorching flame, a stench of a belly the size of Lawrence clearing the way for its human meal—

And she awakened, sitting up in bed, staring.

Staring at two naked women perched on the mattress, on either side of her, *touching* her.

"Sister," whispered Livy, moving her hand higher on Lami's thigh, squeezing.

"Join us," Daria called, still timorous of manner but equally determined, reaching around Lamia to cup her breasts. "Love us, accept us as your family." Her mouth pressed against Lamia's neck, moved to the sweet realm below the ear, and softly sucked. For an insane and impossible moment Lamia thought to herself, *Great Diana's quiver, they're vampires too!*

Livy's fingers teasingly caressed the depths of her belly, above the pubic hair and Lamia realized groggily that these young women must have drugged her food at dinner, intentionally leaving her unable to reach into the creative recesses of her mind for defense. She felt wobbly, only partly conscious and, when she tried to speak, couldn't. Livy was closest, with her mane of yellow hair swept to the front and only her long, protruding nipples showing in the fine golden strands. Her lips were full and wet as her tongue continually lapped them. Her eyes, Lamia saw with vague wisdom, were like those of the monster she'd seen in the nightmare abyss. Eyes of something that could never be entirely satisfied but went on trying with a lunatic kind of persistent valor, always ready to strive again for that which might one day bring release.

She could not see Daria, who sat behind her, except for the little-girl knees oddly pressed close together. And even with the brunette's gentle fingers closing on her high breasts, flicking the nuclei of them, something deep inside Lamia felt sorry for the young woman's vulnerability, her lack of will to venture out in quest of what she might herself have preferred.

Smothering, that was how it felt. There was something hotly suffocating and musky, an overpowering command, to the bosoms that pressed against her back and drifted ever closer to her dry lips. "There'll be no pain, sweet Lamia," came the blonde's husky tones, lifting one breast now as if offering a delicious apple. "Only the ideal love that exists between sisters of the same flesh."

Lamia blinked several times, *willed* herself to act, to cry out—but nothing happened. Now Livy had taken her limp hand, moved it slowly, determinedly, between her own parting legs. She tried to pull it away and found that she lacked the strength, mentally as well as physically. It was as if she'd never awakened from the nightmare, now, and perhaps, perhaps she was still truly asleep. Perhaps it was nothing but a silly, bizarre dream and there was no reason to fight against it anymore because she would merely awaken soon and know it lacked all meaning. With the motion of someone unconscious and deliciously drowning in waters that stole all feeling away, Lamia's body began slipping down in the bed and her head was cradled in Daria's soft, eager lap.

The door of Lamia's bedroom slammed against the wall like a cannon shot, almost splintering. Light from the corridor beyond spilled into the room, catching the three women transfixed on the bed as if frozen in a pornographic photograph.

A great figure stood there, equally immobile, its shadow on the wall in the distant hallway a vaulting, vaunted mass of immense blackness no eye could pierce. The shadow seemed to the women almost to halo the figure. It was like the bleak soul-aura of something huge, and probably corrupt; something that stared in at the lurid scene with blazing, baleful eyes and the punitive heart of a hanging judge.

Daria cried out in surprise and terror. Livy released Lamia's hand and leapt to her feet, one palm across her hairiness. Lamia's head lolled off the brunette's lap and, though she tried to call out, she couldn't.

Then the creature at the door was turning on the lights and Frank Triladus stood some dozen feet from the bed, his flashing eyes judgmental and cold. He wore a tent-like robe that reached the floor and made him look immense, somehow, with his tight-curled head like that of the young Zeus. Dignified, stern, violent and handsome. His lips were pressed together in a grimness that broached no objection and, when he moved his arms in the great enfolding robe, the muscles of his biceps stood out like rocks piled at the barricade of an ancient offensive.

*"She is my woman,"* he said tightly, the voice a bass rumble like that of thunder drawn from a teeming nightsky. *"Get out and never bother her again!"*

Wordless, the sisters, light and dark, gathered up the clothing they'd left just inside the door and scurried into the corridor. They left the door open behind them in their haste and then, down the hallway, there was the angry, frustrated slam of another door.

For a long time Doctor Frank Triladus looked down at the bare Lamia. She was conscious, but barely so, and, he judged unharmed. Her ebony hair spread like the wings of delicate blackbirds over the pillow. Her expression, though sleepy, was grateful and her lips parted faintly in a smile. Her breasts, the sweeping curve of her belly and the fully-revealed black thatch between her long, graceful legs held his gaze for half a minute. He said one word to her and it might have been a prayer: "Somehow."

Then, without approaching her, Triladus wheeled, charged out of the door, and closed it behind him. Lamia heard the sound of a key turning in a lock, then heard it whisked out of the keyhole. There was the sound of male feet moving off down the corridor and Lamia frowned. She was locked in.

It didn't matter. The last thing she thought before drifting into unconsciousness consisted of four, small words: *She is my woman.* Lamia smiled happily in her sleep.

Empty the haunted air, and gnomed
    mine—
Unweave a rainbow, as it erewhile made
The tender-person'd Lamia melt into a
    shade.

               —Keats, *Lamia*

# IX

Lamia awakened early, as usual, stretching luxuriously, pleased that the drug only seemed to have rested her. But she stayed where she was, thinking.

It was possible, anyway, that the door was still locked. Not that she remained in bed for that reason. There were very few doors that could keep Lamia inside, she knew, if she really wanted to get out. But ripping it off its hinges was an act that would only bring questions; questions about a strength which she'd always had to conceal.

Instead of escaping, Lamia had on her mind the warm remembrance of what Frank Triladus said about her to the sisters. Somehow it still sounded delicious in the light of day, becoming someone's "woman" after decades of being primarily alone. Vrukalakos never considered her that way, she knew. To that cruel and oft repulsive vampire she'd been a sort of combination secret sister and roommate-confidante. Fundamentally, she'd meant nothing to him at all.

Modern women, of course, with their lofty sights set on absolute independence from men, would undoubtedly resent being the "woman" of any man, anywhere. Lamia understood that but could not look on it the same way. It seemed to her, as she arose and began combing her long hair, that a man who felt that way about her was simply being macho-sentimental, gloweringly confessing his deeply-sensed commitment. His eagerness, indeed, to protect her against whatever happened to be a threat; his desire to guard their relationship.

The archeologist would not, of course, have any reason to protect Lamia Zacharius! She smiled, considering the absurdity of the notion. She'd always been able to look out for herself where physical danger was concerned. But he did not know about her extraordinary powers and his affection was something Lamia appreciated at that moment in her life.

What bothered her, however, was the cold fact that in almost no sense of the word was there any

126

kind of genuine relationship. Not of an intimate nature, anyway. Until he'd entered the room at midnight to throw Livy and Daria out, saving her from their further sexual blandishments, Triladus had behaved entirely as an employer. She had begun wanting him, privately, weeks ago. But she'd felt that while he might unspokenly lust after her, he basically saw her only as a psychic and an employee.

All of which meant there were many things to consider this bright November day of cool sun streaming in the window, giving her naked olive skin an appearance of glowing. She began to dress, trying to accustom herself to a modern sweater and blue jeans, and faced a problem that was history's oldest challenge to any female. What was she to do about the fact that Mila Triladus existed?

Killing her sounded practical, even rather amusing, but it rubbed Lamia's old-fashioned standards the wrong way. It was unsporting, since Mila might be big as a house but gave the impression of being no more aggressive or strong than the average ordinary woman. She thought it over until she was fully dressed and ready to go downstairs. Finally she had an idea. Mila Triladus was painfully superstitious. Why, then, couldn't her own silly weaknesses be used against her psychologically?

The door was unlocked and Lamia went out

into the hallway and followed the faded carpeting to the stairs. She started to descend, then realized that her unlocked door meant that Frank was already up and around. She couldn't frighten Mila properly in the archeologist's presence.

Instead of going downstairs she retreated down the corridor to Mila's room, and rapped gently on the door. "Enter," came a call from inside and, smiling at the way the woman replied, Lamia opened it and went in.

At least six weeks remained of Mila's pregnancy but, at a glance, the tall woman might have been due that day. She greeted Lamia in a voluminous maternity dress which might have cloaked a baby elephant. She'd washed her hair and it clung to her small head, giving the impression that a careless or unskilled sculptor had used up most of his clay making her body and settled for a little wad for the head.

"I apologize for what I said last night," Mila began promptly. "Sit down there and let me explain."

For an instant Lamia had no idea what the woman meant. Then she remembered Mila's anguished remark suggesting that Lamia had "taken everything else" and could at least leave her with her beliefs. "There's no need, Mila," she said. "Your husband and I haven't done a thing we're ashamed of." She spoke the truth as far as she cared to express it. "Nothing has happened

128

between us at all."

Mila sat on the edge of her bed, the springs squeaking in protest. She seemed to have stuck an over-inflated basketball beneath her skirt. Yet her eyes were soft and she still seemed on the verge of tears. "I'm sure that's true. I was being silly. The books I read tell me that there's nothing unusual about a pregnant woman, all out-of-shape and gross, being worried about other women." She paused, then added cryptically. "Actually, I have no right to oppose Frank in his choice of—of friends, anyway."

"You have every right," Lamia said with warmth. "You're his wife aren't you?"

Mila didn't answer. She seemed to have wandered, lost the thread of their conversation, peering moodily out the window at trees turned brown and crisp. "I never really get used to being away from Greece. We were born there, you know, all four of us."

Lamia hesitated. "So was I," she said at last. "Mila, when does the doctor say you're due?"

The small head spun to face her, the piqued expression on Mila's face defying Lamia to question her. "I haven't gone to one. I'm proud of being an old-fashioned person and I—I just *know* the child will be born very close to Christmas." She finished, vaguely, "A watchful mother knows things like that."

"But where are you having the child?"

"Here." She patted the bed and Lamia realized, for the first time, that its legs were reinforced. "Right here, where it was conceived." Abruptly, she bit her lower lip and lowered her gaze. "I know all mothers are worried about their first l-little ones, but I have a terrible feeling the baby may not be—normal."

Lamia paused. An idea was forming at the back of her mind and, though she hadn't analyzed it, she said what came into her head.

"Mila, do you remember—the *Kallikantzaroi?*"

Mila's head lifted and her eyes stared into the vampire's. "I've heard of it. It—it has something to do with children, doesn't it?" She swallowed. "With—abnormal children?"

Lamia rose from the chair and went to the window, pulling back the curtains to look outside. The skies were black with clouds, themselves pregnant with winter's afterbirth of endless snow. "In the old days when a Greek couple was to have a child born at Christmas they were terrified. It meant that the baby was conceived on March 25th, the Feast of the Annunciation in the Christian religions, when an angel told the Virgin Mary that she would bear Jesus. Do you recall?"

Mila hadn't taken her gaze from Lamia. Her hand started to tremble. "Yes," she said in a whisper, "I recall."

"Such a frightened couple took serious . . . measures . . . to prevent their Christmas baby from turning into a *Kallikantzaros*. A living goblin, Mila." She met the other woman's gaze and held it. "Of course, this is just a silly myth. I'm certain modern science would deride such absurdity, but our people used to believe it. When the child was born, you remember, it was strapped down and smeared with garlic. Sometimes the mother held it tight so the father could approach the infant with fire and . . . *singe* the toenails." She shrugged. "It was better than letting the baby become—something impossibly ugly, and deformed. Malformed."

"What did such children look like, Lamia?" Mila inquired, curious despite herself.

"They looked ghastly, according to the myth." For the first time she realized why she was telling this pregnant woman a story that would scare her badly. Unconsciously, she'd wanted to frighten Mila into a natural abortion. Because a sweet, helpless infant was capable of drawing Mila and Frank—*her* Frank, Lamia considered him—closer together. But now that she realized her unconscious motivations, Lamia wanted to drop the topic. "It was just a silly story."

"Lamia, damn it, I asked you! What does the *Kallikantzaroi child look like?*"

"Some grow so quickly that their waists are level with the rooftops, giant-sized and deadly." Lamia cursed her own impulse in bringing it up but decided to say it all as quickly as possible.

131

"They all have huge heads, they're black and hairy all over, and their eyes are always bloodshot." She made herself laugh. "Part of the nonsense, thousands of years ago, held that a *Kallikantzaros* spent most of the year chopping with an axe at the tree which holds up the world. That's how ridiculous it all is, Mila. Why don't we change the subject now?"

"The rest of it," Mila said grimly. "You and I know some of those stupid trimmings were added, later, by people who wanted us to abandon our beliefs. The *core* of what we believe. Tell me the rest, please."

"Well, the parents have no choice except to arrange for these terrible children to live underground. But around their birthday, near Christmas, they fly into an awful rage and rush above ground. To create havoc for everybody. During the day, when it's not safe for them," Lamia spoke rapidly, her inflection denying her words, "they hide in filthy, damp places and live on snakes, and worms."

"But when it's dark?" Mila persisted. "What happens then?"

Lamia dropped the curtain back into place and turned, shrugging. "They used to say that the *Kallikantzaroi* emerge from daytime darkness to swarm like animals into the house, ripping everything apart—and killing any normal human beings they encounter." She sighed. "It's said

132

they—*rip people to shreds*. Tear them into little pieces." Now she drifted to the bedroom door, sorry in a way that she had begun discussing such things but glad, too, if it brought Frank Triladus nearer her. "These monster babies can only be stopped by hanging a pig's jaw in the interior of the house or throwing a shoe into the fire—they hate burning leather—or simply seizing them in the daylight and . . . detaching their arms and legs!" She opened the door and made herself finish. "All that remains then is a twitching, youthful body and a face with eyes that can still kill simply by looking at you."

Then, glad to be leaving, Lamia closed the door behind her.

In the room Mila moved to her rocking chair, dropped into it heavily, and cupped her arms round her enormous stomach. "Sweet little baby," she crooned, rocking. "Mila's perfect little child."

Frank Triladus looked up as Lamia entered the laboratory. "Why such an unhappy expression?" His sharp gaze swept her from head to toe. "Is it something with Livy and Daria again?"

"No, I'm all right." She poured black liquid from the archeologist's coffee pot and sat at the table, sipping it. "You know how upset Mila gets these days. I stopped in to say hi before coming downstairs and she—bothers me."

"Well, what happened? Did she accuse you

again, the way she did last night?" His lips were pressed together grimly. "Did she shout at you or call you names?"

Lamia held the steaming coffee cup thoughtfully against her lips and shook her head. "Not really. But—sometimes it's hard, Frank." She sighed, seeming quite helpless all at once. "Sometimes I don't feel that I belong here. Or anywhere."

He went to her where she sat and rested his palms on her shoulders as he looked down into her lovely, dark-skinned face. "You belong with me, Lamia. Wherever I am, that's where you belong—and to whom."

She reached out, putting her arms round his hips and pulling him close. "Then it wasn't a dream, was it—what I heard last night?"

He smiled down at her and caressed the top of her head. "I suppose it was my dream, Lamia, not yours. My dream that you could, indeed, be my woman."

"I am," she whispered. Her fingers found him close to her and she ran the zipper down, reached inside and freed him. She was startled by his size and length when his penis sprung into sight, and she held it momentarily against her cheek. Hot, it was so hot, throbbing with blood. Her tongue flicked practicedly. "I am your woman, Frank," she said in a silvery, almost musical way. He saw her brilliant white teeth shining against her

134

teasing, voluptuous lips. "I shall prove it to you."

Lamia was on her knees, then, deliberate as she arched her neck, licked her lips, and took him in. He made a small sound that might have been the word "don't," except that Lamia could not believe she understood him properly. Looking down, he saw the trace of moisture shining on her moving, scarlet lips, and the archeologist thought wildly that this was somehow familiar, this scene; that it was almost like something he'd read, a long while ago.

Lamia placed her hands, softly, around the generous root which she could not quite encompass, balancing. Slowly, steadily, she began rocking to and fro, a quiet yet aggressive song keening deep in her throat. When next Triladus looked down he seemed to have been devoured by some great, gratifying beast, for all that he could see was her tangle of long, black hair below her waist and, just for an instant, Triladus shut his eyes in languorous ecstasy.

When at last he remembered—when the terrible, agonizing truth occurred to him of what must happen next, the truth that he could never reveal to Lamia—Doctor Frank Triladus abruptly yanked away from her, sharp teeth raking on super-sensitive skin, and dashed awkwardly, pathetically out the laboratory door. Astounded and wounded, Lamia stared after him. Surely she had done it properly; surely he was enjoying it.

135

Yet he had pulled away long before the satisfaction that she had meant fully to give him.

Lamia patted her lips with a tissue, brushed her hair into place, and took a chair at the laboratory table. She poured coffee and, more shaken than she had realized, watched the cup tremble. Nothing made any sense to her anymore. Frank had allowed her, at least for awhile, to make love to him. But he had neither permitted her to finish nor returned the favor. Her body ached for his touch, his caress. Why, Lamia wondered, filled with deep concern, why wouldn't the man who swore she belonged to him make love to her?

. . . And shapeless sights come wandering
    by,
The ghastly people of the realm of dream,
Mocking me: and the Earthquake fiends
    are charged
To wrench the rivets from my quivering
    wounds.
                —Shelly, *Prometheus Unbound*


Tremendous Image, as thou art must be
He whom thou shadowest forth. I am his
    foe,

                        —*Ibid*


Aether, the Titan binds the globe . . ."
                —Empedocles


All hell broke loose.
                —Milton, *Paradise Lost*

# X

"Listen!" she commanded, holding up a hand. "It's so *quiet!*"

He paused with the thermos of coffee in his own hand, doing as she asked, and nodded. When he spoke it was in that soft, almost stealthy way people have of instinctively responding to and respecting the silence of a library. Or a mortuary. "Maybe it's always that way, in the woods. You know, at night."

Kendra shook her head. "I don't really think so, Jack. Shouldn't there be insects in the grass at least?" The pretty woman's black face twisted in concern. "I think there's something out there, watching us. And its presence frightens the animals."

He got his legs under him and pulled himself to his feet, smiling. "Lord, Ken, you'd find something mysterious in a church!" Jack opened the door of the second-hand camper for which he'd saved and scrimped these past ten years and went inside to check on Rosalie. He knew Eddie would be along soon, that he was just finishing up his fishing for the day, but the baby was still too young to go unattended for long. That Eddie, now, was something else. Eight years old and just like his old man, eager to be left on the bank for awhile and prove his manliness to himself.

Jack grinned with pride for his son and looked reflectively at Rosalie, checking her out. The nine-month-old black child was sleeping peacefully, a thumb between her lips. Jack started to pull it out, remembering the constant advice of his mother-in-law. "She'll ruin her mouth if you let her do that, Jack," the old lady had scolded. But Jack didn't really believe it so he simply kissed her sweet forehead before going back outside.

Sometimes a man knows, at once, that something is wrong. The area before the camper was deserted. His wife was nowhere in sight and Jack's heartbeat instantly accelerated.

"Kendra?" he called. No answer. Now where had she gone off to? Surely not far, because Ken wasn't really hot for the woods. They'd never turned her on the way they did him, especially like now when the weather was turning cold. Part of it was the way her old lady filled Kendra's young head with her old-fashioned nonsense. The poor girl figured by now that the KKK was never more'n a hundred yards away, wherever they went. That was why he kept the shotgun in the camper, just to let her know they had protection in case anything went wrong. Jack hadn't fired it once.

"Yo, Ken!" he shouted, frowning because he'd been obliged to break the silence. It made him feel like a trespasser. or a drunk at the funeral home. "Where'd you *go*, Ken? *Kendra!*"

139

Nothing at all stirred. No sound reached him; he waited in a void.

Jack Pike stood stock-still in his heavy sweater, jeans and down jacket in front of his hard-won camper, close to the fire they'd made. It was the only thing he could see clearly at all, and you never really saw a fire clearly because it was a dancing fool. It kept shifting shapes and changing faces as if disguising itself, hoarding its hot secrets to itself. Kendra must-of gone after Eddie, sure, that was it. But if so, the stream wasn't all that far away. 'Less they were playing a joke on him, why didn't they answer . . . Couldn't they hear him?

Once he'd been an all-state tackle from Crispus Attucks High School and maybe some of the weight he carried had begun turning to mush, but Jack Pike knew he was still capable of holding his own with the average man. Black or white, made no difference. Jack couldn't recall ever being scared in his whole life and he liked being Ken and Eddie's and little Rosalie's protector, he liked being there when they needed him, handling a full load of responsibility.

He couldn't remember ever being scared in his whole life. Till now. Everything about the quietude scared hell out of him.

He'd figured if he really listened close—let his athlete's senses go feeling their way into the woods the way he'd captained the team on defense and sensed the signals being called by the offense—he'd be okay. Kendra's answering call or the pounding footsteps of his son Eddie would be right along.

Instead, the awful, quite unnatural quiet deepened. It was something you could almost feel with your skin. The darkness wrapped its unseen arms round him, so thick and heavy Jack half expected to peer down the length of his sturdy body and spy real stars twinkling in the invisible mass that engulfed his waist and chest. *Cosmic*, he thought, recalling the TV series he'd seen with the sharp-witted, aristocratic little white astronomer; *why it's like standing among the stars of the heavens and knowing that one bitty step would put you smack dab in a black hole. Something that compressed all the atoms in your body and quickly reduced you to maybe half an inch of quivering black raspberry jelly. The cosmos, KKK of infinity, asking no questions and changing no answers, 'cause it'd always been that way and simply always would be.*

He went back to the camper, got the shotgun, clacked it open and filled it with mean red shells. When he got back outside he turned and looked the door to keep Rosalie safe, told himself what a fool he was getting to be. *If I see a white sheet I'll probably yell, Feets, do yer stuff* . . . Pulling a flashlight from his jacket pocket, he ventured into the woods.

He hadn't gone far when he stopped, eyes

bulging, mouth agape. The stream where his son Eddie and he were fishing—wasn't there! He froze, more perplexed than horrified. The ground was damp, strewn with dead or dying fish. Lord, it was like some fantastic Abominable Snowman had plunked into the creek and, whoosh! slammed out all the water.

He poked the beam from his flashlight. There, here, there. Yes, there—something out of place. Something that didn't belong there at all. He jogged over to it and stooped, hand trembling, to retrieve Eddie's tennis shoe. Eddie wasn't in it. Very slowly, with great care and an awful semi-knowledge filling his belly with the kind of terror that sometimes paralyzes, Jack Pike put the shoe in his pocket and threw the light down a trail to the east. Here, the trees lifted like dark columns with all the dignity of a mad and murdering monarch. They looked like etchings he'd seen, hard pencil sketches, not like anything real. Jaws grimly set, he edged his way out of the clearing into the path and felt immediately swallowed up by more than silence, more somehow than even the cosmos had to offer. Naked among the stars, he'd still seen the universe around him. Here, there was only the pale, prodding lifeline of the flashlight beam—

And then, for the first time, sounds. The sounds, Jack thought with a freezing shiver of fear, of bones crunching.

Maybe Ken got past him somehow, he thought without believing it, maybe she was already back at the camper. He turned away from the trail, suddenly acutely aware of a warning sent directly from his shriveling soul, a frigid resistive sensible for-God's-sake-don't-go-there kind of message that made him want indeed to move his silly feet. To run—run as he'd never run before—for the relative safety of his beloved camper. But a man, a football star, didn't do that till he knew. Where was Eddie? Where the hell was Kendra?

His spine stiffened and he didn't move a muscle. *Something* was behind him, hovering above his head like a massing of vicious thunder-clouds holding a personal vendetta against hard-working black family men. He took a breath. With the shotgun slowly rising until he had it at man's chest level, Jack Pike turned back to the trail and the woods surrounding it.

He saw the front legs first, bigger around than the trunks of the largest trees, planted in his path. *Rooted* there, it appeared, like defiant redwoods. He worked his tortured gaze up then to the impossible, scaly chest, itself a nearly unending expanse of armored and leathery skin that forced its way among the oaks and elms by splintering them down the middle. Now there was sound, not only of trees becoming instant grist for the papermills but the unutterably loathsome, quasi-human sound of the great monster Aether, breathing.

Branches trembled at the force of expelled air and he felt the foul stench on the top of his head, gagged at its putrescence. Finally Jack looked all the way up, and screams of horror and disbelief were momentarily throttled by a vaster sense of heartstricken awe—

Until he saw the flame red, bizarrely intelligent eyes, and until he saw the massive planet that was Aether's head and what orbited limply from its rending, blood-soaked maw.

She was beyond human help. Jack knew it at once, much the way one knows he will be racked with heart pains or devouring cancer someday, or knows he must rot forever in the earth. Fear made him face the fact of Kendra's hideous demise that quickly, although with a rent of loss no less grief-stricken for its compact registering on his brain, and he fired the shotgun anyway. Both barrels ripped into the thing before him in a scarlet singeing flare, and when the monster just blinked at him, he ran. His old athlete legs dug fiercely into the ground the way they had when he chased a fleet scatback from Gary Roosevelt, years ago, in a state championship game. But the outcome of *this* contest, the prize awaiting him if he could win, was nothing short of his life on earth and quite possibly the raked tatters of his staggered sanity.

One subject filled Jack's mind as he broke into the clearing and saw the hulking camper ahead, with only the dwindling fire to pass before he reached safety. Tiny, helpless Rosalie, his motherless child. Did he dare take the time to unlock the camper door, get in, and start the motor? Or would the little girl be safer if he skirted the vehicle and plunged headlong down the road for help?

The indecision of his thinking cost Jack Pike dearly. Fumbling for his keys, he dropped them in the grass in front of the camper and, moaning low in his throat, fell to his knees to look for them. The fire was almost out and the first thing he thought was his keys proved to be a glittering cigarette tinfoil. After that, there was no more time.

Aether, the Titan, hadn't bothered to run. Aether walked faster, covered ground more quickly, than a swift man could run. Aether wasn't disturbed by fear or concern, but was only mildly slowed by curiosity and some remnant of prudence left over from a time when armored men on horseback jabbed him with lances. Aether . . . was *there*, above him, when Jack looked up.

A single massive foot lifted, beclawed with nails like the blades soldiers kept in scabbards, raised it higher than a tall man stood and then came crunchingly down. Jack saw it coming, realized that its bulk and speed made swift human motion anachronistic. The foot struck him on top of his curly black head, passed directly through the

145

brain and, unslowed, simply pressed Jack into the dirt. The way a man might squash an irksome, buzzing insect.

There wasn't even enough left to twitch.

Silence descended again as Aether listened briefly, head larger than a motorcycle sidecar against the background of Thessaly's trees. Then the oddly-small, handlike projections that could have reminded a calm person of the fearful "arms" of Tyrannosaurus rex reached into the dirt to scoop up what remained of Jack Pike. With his food halfway to his gaping mouth, Aether again paused to listen, staring eyes hostile and wary. What he heard was the sound of a human baby, crying. From inside the vehicle, Aether realized, annoyed at being interrupted in his meal taking.

Casually, even negligently, the great beast turned his spiny back on the huge camper and lashed out once with his massive graybrown tail. It hit the camper with the instant whumppp! of an explosion, bending it nearly double and sending it rolling over and over. When it reached the highway, spinning on its ruined front wheels, it careened in front of an oncoming semi and the night was no longer black or quiet.

Soaring walls of flame crimsoned the air. Automobiles behind the semi fought frantically to swerve. Two made it. More failed, colliding with the burning mess. More flames belched skyward. Sections of man's pet machine shot across each

146

side of the road, carving into other vehicles and other flesh. There was eerie silence for a moment. Then, at a distance, the siren call of authority wailed like a lost soul.

For some time Aether watched as he chewed, intrigued by what was happening. His immense eyes rarely blinked. *He'd* done this; one flip of his tail had caused this marvelous show. Aether ran a femur the width of his mouth, neatly cleaning the bone, and in the fiery inferno and lunatic shadows looked like a psychotic's image of Buddha dining on chicken. When his eye finally shut, once, it was a regal acknowledgment of how much he'd enjoyed the fun. An ugly parody of a human smile formed as Aether settled down to watch the rest of it. Later he would return to the woods to plan his first intentional attack on civilization in thousands of years. He could scarcely wait.

Meanwhile, a terrified little boy named Eddie Pike burst into a police station on the outskirts of Indianapolis. When he could talk again, he broadcast the news: All hell had just broken loose.

Lamia first learned that Aether was definitely out of the cave to Antipodes when Livy and Daria discussed it at dinner that night. Neither of them had mentioned their failed effort to involve Lamia in lesbianism and she, already bouyed by Frank's admission that he loved her and wishing only peace, let it go too.

147

Tonight, however, she was horrified and disgusted by the way Livy made light of Aether. "'Gigantic monster,' indeed!" she laughed merrily, touching Daria's forearm. "Did you ever hear anything so silly in your life?"

"Maybe Indianapolis decided to do its own version of the old Orson Welles 'War of the Worlds,'" the small brunette replied with a fresh grin.

"Why not?" Livy asked loftily. "This place has always been fifty years behind the rest of civilization anyway."

Frank Triladus tapped nervously on the edge of his water glass. "I heard the radio report too," he said softly, looking concerned. His glance flitted to Lamia. "There's to be some film on television later, I understand."

"Oh, come on, Frank!" Livy pleaded, arching her pale brows. "You're a scientist now, for God's sake!" She touched his hairy wrist. "Surely you don't believe a genuine *dragon* decided to pay Indianapolis a visit!"

"In San Francisco or New Orleans, maybe," Daria put in. "Maybe it's here early to qualify for the 500 Mile Race!"

"It's hard to believe," Triladus said, looking at both Lamia and Mila with a wry half-smile, "that these two used to be the psychics of the family. There was a time when I thought I'd be able to use their skills in my work, Lamia. But they've gone

148

ultra-modern on us. Two little materialists determined to do their thing."

"I had no idea they were sensitives too," Lamia
said, surprised, staring at the sisters. "What form
did it take?"

"Livy was the best at projecting telepathic
images I ever saw," Triladus replied. "Daria was
always so attuned to Livy they could communicate halfway round the world if they needed to."

"Let's not talk about that," Livy said with a
scowl. Then she brightened. "I'll bet I know
what's in the woods at Thessaly! The world's first
genuine male chauvinist pig—a real hog gone
mad! Probably a prize winner at the State Fair for
some hick Hoosier farmer feeding it a combination of discarded wives and—and masculine bull-
shit!"

Mila looked pale and frightened. "What d-did
the creature in the woods do? Did it hurt someone?"

Lamia looked at her from beneath half-lowered
lids. "It killed a man named Jack Pike and his
wife. Apparently it ate them alive. After the thing
went back into the woods they found pieces of
clothing. And human bones picked clean."

"Ate them?" Mila stared numbly at Lamia. Her
voice was a whisper. "Picked clean?" She
touched her rumbling abdomen.

"Poor thing," Livy said blithely. "The people
probably gave it awful indigestion."

"For God's sake, *shut up!*" Triladus rose from the table and tossed down his napkin, glowering at Livy. "You tasteless bitch, don't you realize that it must be Aether, that he's found another damnable exit?"

Lamia gaped openly at him as he brushed past the others, then paused beside her. He touched her arm. "I'll explain later. Aether is a mystical beast from antiquity and he—he fits this thing's description." He smiled briefly at her and stomped out of the room.

Moments later, Lamia also rose. "Excuse me," she said, unable to bear being alone with the sisters.

In her room, Lamia puzzled for several minutes about Frank's knowledge of Aether and concluded that given his special professional interests and ambitions, it wasn't unusual at all for him to know about the creature. Yet it surprised her to see his passion. As a scientist, he might have been expected to scoff at the possibility of Aether's genuine existence.

She took several objects from Frank's chest and arranged them on her bed. The sooner she went through them all, displaying her psychometric accuracy, the sooner she could tell him that the answer to his search for the missing link awaited them in the Himalayas. Once there, she would locate Demogorgon and persuade him to return with them in order to slay Aether.

But just as importantly, Lamia thought with a secret smile, once they were away from this madhouse at last, Frank would finally be willing to share their love. It was, like everything, only a matter of time. And Lamia possessed time in abundance.

For it is unknown what is the real nature
of the soul, whether it be born with the
bodily frame or be infused at the moment
of birth . . . or whether it visits the shades
of Pluto and bottomless pits, or enters by
divine appointment into other animals.
                                                    —Lucretius


We are steaming up from Hell's wide gate
And we burthen the blast of the
        atmosphere . . .
And the inarticulate people of the dead,
Preserve, a treasured spell.
                        —Shelley, *Prometheus Unbound*


## XI


During the night Lamia stirred restlessly in her
sleep, tossed back the covers from her naked
beauty, then sat bolt upright with her luminous
eyes staring dismally into the blackness. The
window across the way seemed to swell as the

curtains blossomed with November air; outside the night was starless and the wind whipping at her body drew Lamia's nipples erect.

When she realized what had awakened her she lowered her forehead to her knees and tried not to weep. She rarely did anymore; it was as if nature portioned out her tears to human beings and, after a few hundred years, gave no more. She shook her head, trying to ignore the feeling—her great need—and swiftly, grimly realized that even her loving fascination for Frank Triladus could not take precedence over her nature's special demands.

Because of her retroactive feelings about the sadistic pimp whom she so recently killed, the vampire attack hadn't taken. She was left uptight and feeling hollow, vaguely jittery and on edge. The deeply-born, horrific requirements of the vampire were always more subtle, more psychologically oriented, than most ordinary people understood. In a queer, off-putting kind of way, the blood thirst of her kind was strangely romantic, akin to the stern demands of sex.

Whenever a night of making love was unfulfilling, when one did not climax or feel the release created from mutual need and mutual expression, it sometimes left a woman off key and unsatisfied until the next chance arose to make love. And so it was for vampires, as well.

While Lamia Zacharius gave the appearance

always of rare, haughty beauty and a serene, sophisticated kind of self-control, she was more like a college freshman who kept her sorority aspiring nose in the air to keep from trembling. There remained in Lamia's private heart some final traces of the puny, poor, great-eyed child she had once been in the streets of ancient Greece. An orphan, hungrier more times than not, even more starving for affectionate hugs and kind words, she had lacked all self-assurance until Vrukalakos introduced her to Pythagoras. Together, while they might have placed her soul in mortal jeopardy, they had given her not only a prolonged life but the exceptional needs of society's vampires.

In addition to the ways she retained as a female. To this night, Lamia admitted to herself as she rose from bed to dress simply in sweater and slacks, it wasn't really good for her unless it was good for the man she attacked. Always she hungered for her forays to be more than mere vampirization, to prove mutually fulfilling, and they so seldom were.

But for the life of her Lamia couldn't understand why that was so. There was an immense intimacy at the moment she leaned against a man and locked her teeth in his throat, a closeness when bubbles of blood from the dual bites began to flow, and when she lapped it up like a neat housekitten that seemed to her nearer and more private than mere sexuality. Sex itself depended upon the hidden genitals. The eternal lovemaking of vampires involved the organs of speech, kissing and the snowwhite fangs which devoured life-sustaining food, not to mention the arteries that throbbed from the heart itself.

Sometimes, when they did not struggle, Lamia would even kiss and soothe them, cradle those heads in her soft arms that were closer to death than they'd ever been before, providing succor in much the same way a good nurse worked, even promising afterlife rewards which she herself might never know. So many of her victims over the centuries were Christians, after all, who claimed to believe in a beautiful heavenly here-after. If that was so, perplexed Lamia wondered, why did they thrash so much to keep from going to a better world?

Rarely, however, there was that sensitive, perceptive male victim who managed to look her in the eyes with gratitude at the moment she tore out his throat to feast. These were the times that made everything worthwhile, when she felt most like a woman, and most like a vampire. Some-times Lamia would twitch the whole length of her body with the shiver of fulfilled desire, and hold the dead man close to her own heart, envying him for the marvelous, long journey he had begun. *She* did that, Lamia would think with pride; it began with her aid, her kind direction, and release.

155

As she tiptoed through the house and drifted like a slender shadow into the early-winter night, she hoped that this would prove to be a night to remember. Willing it, seeking speed and alacrity, she became a beautiful sleek female dog—a shepherd, they'd say with their idle glances; how handsome—trotting swiftly down the silent streets of Lawrence, west into neighboring Indianapolis.

Clearly, she thought, that part of the big city near downtown was weird and uncivilized. She would not go so far this time; she would settle for the North Eastwood shopping mall and find her victim there.

Lamia turned west off North Post Road into the parking area and, red tongue languidly drooping from her mouth, passed a Fox Photo kiosk, the charming neighborhood library, a furniture store and a place that sold hardware. Light puddled the entrance to Hook Drugs and she sat on her temporary haunches, waiting to see who would emerge.

Two children exited, a boy and a girl, digging with grubby fingers in their brown sacks for candy. Lamia ignored them. An old lady slowly trudged her way into the street moments later and Lamia's gaze followed her to an idling car and an elderly gentleman at the wheel. A handsome young man with a name tag reading "Tony" stuck his head out, clapped his palms and cried "Shoo!"; but when she licked his hand, he went back inside with a smile. Then there was a long wait.

Finally, looking through the glass doors, she saw her target for the night. He was standing by the cash register, paying for cigarettes, and Lamia's heart beat more quickly. Tall, lanky, blue-eyed with a beard, dressed in a waist length coat and jeans, the man couldn't have been over twenty-two or twenty-three, and her nose grew warmer. When he came out, missing a step and stumbling slightly, Lamia thought for a moment that he was drunk, and backed away. A closer look and a quick smell with her transient, canine nostrils told her differently. There was a faint, sweet fragrance about him, but it wasn't alcohol.

Instead of getting into a car, the young man began walking, passing a *Radio Shack,* a health spa, and a *Zale's Jewelers.* He didn't keep striding toward the sprawling *Kroger* supermarket but turned left into the mall itself. Quietly, casually, Lamia trotted after him. He didn't seem to see her at all.

When she followed him, she learned that the mall was almost dark, the few stores doing business there already closed for the night. She could see light at the other end and expected him to pass through the mall. But again, he surprised her.

Lamia's padding feet stopped, forepaw in the air, as she watched him step into a darkened

157

doorway and saw a match flicker. Ah, he was lighting a cigarette or cigar! And this, clearly—semi-darkness, no open stores, no other people in sight—was the place to attack. She took five steps and on the fifth was herself again: tall, statuesque, beautiful and womanly.

"That's a nice trick," the young man said as she approached. His tone was approving, devoid of surprise or fear. "Usually I get flashes like that only on LSD."

Lamia didn't reply. She just kept walking, toward him, seeing both how handsome he was and how strangely his turquoise eyes glinted in the shadows.

"In case it turns out later you're real," he said affably, sucking hard on his cigarette and pinching it between his fingers, "they call me York. And you are like gorgeous."

Just for an instant Lamia's step hesitated. The young man sounded so serious and he was so perfect she couldn't believe her eyes. It would be a pleasure to bite his neck, to see those fine blue eyes catch a glimpse of eternity. She was within arm's length, then, her smile challenging.

"Is this a vision with a name," he asked lightly, leaning against the store, "or without? Either way, it's fine. If you don't have one, I'll give you a name, so I can remember you when I come down. Okay?"

"My name is Lamia," she said and, when she

was very near, he parted his arms so that she could step into them. "You're very pretty, York." His own lips were inches away. "A handsome boy."

York giggled. "Man, where did I get this stuff! You can really get off on grass like this." He kissed her full mouth, prodded between her lips for her tongue.

Lamia felt his groin growing hot and heavy against her and, as she moved her mouth from his lips to the side of his neck she also rested her hand over his swelling manhood. "I'm so glad I found you," she whispered. "So grateful." At the moment her hand squeezed, and began to move, she bit deeply into his throat.

"S'all right," he replied, showing no indication that he'd experienced pain. "Glad to be of small service." He laughed a little and cupped her breast with his hands, one below and one on top. It looked as if he might be trying to pick up a heavy grapefruit. "Hey, think nothin' of it!"

Lamia paused, startled by his reaction. Just about now York was supposed to be sliding down the side of the building, dying. Instead, he was working his fingers under her sweater and trying, rather mildly, to lift it over her head.

She ignored his hands even as the bottom of the sweater gathered around her throat and again fastened her incisors deep in his neck, lower, closer to the jugular. "Crazy," he said off-

159

handedly. "Far out."

Just as she was beginning to bat at his hands to keep from being undressed in the middle of a shopping center, York gave her a crazy, handsome smile and dumped himself on the sidewalk. She dropped to her knees beside him, lapping at the wound in his throat, seeing the weird light in his eyes begin to fade away.

"Soon," she said tenderly, under his ear, "soon you will be walking in green pastures."

"All right!" he said agreeably, blinking.

"Friends and family members you've not seen in years will come out to greet you."

"That's cool, too," he replied, sighing a little and folding his hands together in his lap. He was gratefully relaxed; there wasn't a shred of struggle and, it occurred to Lamia, there hadn't been much consciousness to begin with. "Right on."

"You'll hear heavenly music," she told him softly, her lips working, sucking now, "the loveliest sounds you ever heard."

"Hey, mama," he said groggily, leaning his handsome head against her shoulder, "one thing: D'they have festival seating?"

Moments later Lamia stood, lost her balance, caught it on the store building. Her head was reeling. When she looked toward the entrance to the mall there were hundreds of lights, instead of a few, and when she squinted to pick out the right ones, they spelled out: "Lamia Zacharius! In Person This Week Only!" Annoyed with herself, she willed herself to become a shepherd again.

Nothing happened except a little shuddery feeling that made her giggle. Lamia couldn't remember the last time she'd giggled. It was so much fun, she did it again. Then she imagined herself a fleet white rabbit and, instead of turning into one, saw a little pink-nosed bunny in a top hat dash nimbly across her path.

It was a long walk back to Lawrence.


Two days later Lamia had tape recorded the remainder of her psychometric findings from Frank Triladus' trunk and discovered, to her wondering amazement, that she would not have to lie: Frank's missing link was unquestionably last encountered in south central Asia, on the border of Tibet and India, in a range of mountains extending more than two thousand miles: the Himalayas.

She was delighted that she would not have to lie to the curly-haired archeologist but for the first time troubled about locating Demogorgon once she was there. The Himalayas formed the highest and most rugged mountain barrier in the world, cutting off India to the south from the remainder of Asia to the north. It was here that James Hilton had imagined his wondrous Shangri-La, here that Tibetans welcomed Alexandra David-Neal and shared with westerners the knowledge of how to create a living being, called a *tulpa*. Here, too, the Abominable Snowman was said to cavort ten thousand feet above sea level or among the monsoon forests and the swamp-tracked jungle of Terai. Even after the arrival of the Chinese, large areas of the Himalayas remained totally unpopulated, presumably never visited by man. The lines of communication were primarily roads traversing the Khyber Pass and the connecting towns to Pakistan, plus the railroad at Rawalpindi. Other passage was possible only along incredibly precarious mountain trails.

When she'd candidly told Frank all she knew, Lamia flushed with happiness at his immediate response. He'd held her hand and said, smilingly: "We'll leave for there right after Mila has her child. Just the two of us, my beautiful Lamia, alone at the top of the world."

At dinner that night Livy was disconcerting. She gave Lamia the impression of trying to decipher her ill-disguised buoyancy. At length, Frank, too, seemed to sense the blonde's efforts and boldly broke the news.

"Lamia has proved as indispensable to my plans as I'd hoped she would, right from the start," he announced. He touched Mila's plump hand and gave her a gentle smile. "After your little one comes, Lamia and I will leave for the Himalayas. I think this may prove to be the end to our quest. In

162

a day or two we'll look into travel accommodations."

Mila returned his smile and then turned her head to meet her sister's steady, solemn gaze. As Lamia watched, Livy smiled at Mila, at last, and nodded.

She forgot about it when she was opening her bedroom door and found Frank himself slipping from the shadows of the old house to put his arms around her waist. "That rarefied air," he said cryptically, his nose and lips muzzled in her black hair, "that's what we need. We'll be together soon, my dearest."

Then he was holding her in his arms so tightly it hurt, but the pain was oddly welcome, the kind of close kin to romance that every lover comes to know. His mouth was hard on hers, rough but exciting, and when he stepped back to leave her there Lamia found herself blinking after his disappearing bulk with the feverish, undisciplined eyes of a teenager.

Going to sleep was difficult, but when she drifted off, finally, Lamia was smiling to herself.

It didn't last.

The door flew open, causing her to jump into a seated position on the bed, shaking, as her lips parted in consternation and astonishment.

*Vrukalakos, the swarthy and saturnine vampire who'd been her closest peer in Thessaly's synod, stepped quickly into the room. Lamia stared. Behind*

163

*him came Pythagoras himself, the wonderful old man still a wiser St. Nicholas in his white mane and curling beard. Young Andruss was there, Reverend Bandrocles, even the obese and ugly sisters Mormo and Sybaris. Trailing the group were the others from Thessaly's governing Syndic: Nicholas Melas and hairless George Aristides. They were* alive!

"*She-devil!*" Vrukalakos cried, stepping close enough to strike her across the cheek. It smarted badly and she fell back. "You left me to die in *pieces*, before Aether's cave! You did *nothing* to save me!"

"Patience, patience," murmured the stocky Patriarch, stepping in front of the angry vampire. He tugged disconsolately at his beard. "Let us hear her explanation, *Dios Kodion!*" His eyes burned into hers. "*Why*, daughter, did you not join your *phrateres* in Antipodes? Can you understand that they felt . . . abandoned?"

Lamia nodded, looking with pain from one familiar face to another. Once these people were her only family. "There was no one else, with Vrukalakos gone, who c-could be saved but me." She gasped a quick breath. "It made no sense to be devoured by Aether when, even then, I should continue to live as a mottled scrap of his food."

"We were friends, Lamia," young Andruss said, his handsome face sad. When he drew nearer she felt a pang as she saw the claw marks on his cheek. Her knuckles went to her lips. "When you

164

posed as Lythia, to help us win Mary Graham's cooperation, I looked upon you as my sister. But you, Lamia, deserted me!"

"I didn't, Andruss, I didn't!" She put her hands on his sturdy shoulders, beseechingly. "You were all determined to follow the Patriarch into the Vale of Aphaca. I could not dissuade you! It was foolishness to perish in such a way!"

"Foolishness?" asked one fat sister, Sybaris.

"Or loyalty?" demanded the other, moving closer. Mormo's hands doubled into fists. She hissed the word: "Bitch!"

"Wait, my *akousmatokoi*," called the old man, "wait! She may yet have an explanation we can understand." He touched Lamia's chin with a finger, virtually pleading. "Did you, perhaps, plan to save the *Logos*, our priceless volume of truth?"

"No," Lamia whispered. "I could not."

"Did you hope to find a few survivors, perhaps," he asked again, the eyes of his genius boring into her, "and rebuild Thessaly elsewhere? Create a third town of Greek wisdom?"

"There were," she said simply, "no survivors."

"That is not true," exclaimed Melad, pointing a finger.

"There was *one!*" shouted Aristides.

That was when they all began inching closer to her. Lamia turned to Reverend Bandrocles, locking her fingers on his arm. "Please, make them understand!" Already Vrukalakos' claws were reaching for her. "Reverend, stop them!"

"I shall pray for your soul, daughter," Bandrocles intoned solemnly, taking a step away from her.

Then they were all atop her, battering her to the floor. Vrukalakos' dripping jaws hung above her throat, ready to rip it asunder. The Mormo sisters straddled her legs, weighting her down. Melas and Aristides loomed overhead, fists knotted, prepared to batter her face. And Pythagoras pulled a knife from inside his snowy robes and raised it, slowly, sadly, above her breast.

*The Patriarch would never kill.* Lamia closed her eyes, kept them that way. *It is unthinkable that Pythagoras would steal a life for anything except metempsychosis, transplanting his soul to another form to remain alive. And Vrukalakos, he was a vampire as was she—and vampires could not enter where they were not asked! It was all mistake, a human mistake!*

When she opened her eyes she was lying drenched in perspiration on the floor, naked and alone. Her room was still. She peered at the door across the room and saw that it remained shut. And there had not been the sound of people leaving.

It was only a nightmare, some terrible vision— *implanted in her brain!*

She pulled her legs under her and came to a

crouch, snarling like an animal. Livy and Daria! Livy somehow using her own private feelings of remorse and guilt against her, the bitch! Playing their amateur psychic games to repay her for failing to become one of them. Or perhaps, she saw it suddenly, to stop her from going with Frank to Asia! To protect their precious giant sister Mila from being left behind!

Livid with rage, Lamia began stalking the room. Her yard-long length of obsidian hair trailed behind her bare, athletic body like the tail of a spirited filly. Occasionally she showed her fanged incisors and saliva flecked her lips. For the first time in decades the rims of her eyes were sunrise-red with rage. As she strode, her fingers were locked like steel claws, scratching at the offensive air which seemed stifling now, threatening, with the knowledge that Livy and Daria were trying to scare her out of the house.

She whirled to face the wall and, seizing a lamp from a nearby table, hurled it with such phenomenal strength that it shattered to a million tiny splinters.

Panting heavily, she continued looking at the wall, knowing that the sisters' room was right down the hall, realizing, as she considered going after them, that they would never let her in now that they had invaded her mind and discovered her secrets. There was no time to lose! They would tell Frank, or Mila, soon—this very day!

Finally Lamia nodded and swept her long hair back with a decided and settled toss of her head. If the sensual blonde and her supplicating little sister wanted to play psychic head-games, more than two could play!

When Frank and his pregnant creature left the house to look into travel accommodations for the trip to the Himalayas, then it would be her move—Lamia's move—in the game.

She made an audible snarling sound at the wall and sat cross-legged on the floor, for all the world a naked Greek Indian planning her attack. This was a game Lamia Zacharius *never* lost . . .

Howl, Spirits of the living and the dead,
Your refuge, your defense lies fallen and
vanguished.
   —Shelley, *Prometheus Unbound*

Then Lamia breath'd death breath . . .
    —Keats, *Lamia*

## XII

Silken, sweating Livy looked up from the bed at her darker-haired sister, gasping with heightened pleasure and anticipation. Daria had paused in her labors to rise above Livy now and, with glazed eyes and red, moistened lips, she returned a sweet and obsequious smile. Livy reached out to cup her palm between Daria's legs, an index finger moving expertly. When Daria dipped her head to kiss the lengthy tips of Livy's bosom, one by one, her hair fanned out on the blonde's thin body like a light and shimmering coverlet. Knowing that even a slave has a measure of power if she knows how to

169

exercise it, Daria ran her middle finger between her sister's uptilted breasts and then down the length of her form, stopping—teasingly, defiantly—caught in a tangle of damp pubic strands. Livy lifted and twisted her buttocks hungrily. "The object," she gasped, gesturing wildly to the nightstand. "Use the object!"

Daria twisted a little on the mattress to put out her hand, trying to pin Livy's and keep it where it was. If she did everything well tonight, if she pleased her autocratic sister in every sensual respect, it might be her turn again.

But as she turned her head, Daria cried out in sudden alarm, staring at the interloper standing just inside the locked bedroom door. "Lamia!" she exclaimed, dropping the vibrator and pointing.

Livy raised her golden head from the pillow to see. Slowly, a deeply pleased, even triumphant smile moved on her wide mouth. Victory! Lamia Zacharius had come to her, after all, and she was even more beautiful than Livy could tell when they were in the sensitive's darkened bedroom. Here the lights were bold and high, revealing everything. And the psychic's breasts were small and compact, high-placed to the point of appearing fresh and virginal. Livy licked her dry lips. Lamia's waist was narrow, the naval a perfect circular indentation above the tight-curled mass of ebony hair. Her hips flared deliciously and the legs, ah, Livy longed to lie with her own head between them, ached to feel them bare and skin-hot round her own broad shoulders.

"Welcome to the family, sweet Lamia," she called in sultry, purring tones. Her eyes were bright and staring. "I'm so glad our little telepathic show changed your mind. Were you so filled with guilt for what you did to your friends that you decided to make a new turn in life?"

Daria, knowing that her own plans were ruined but hoping eventually to be included, climbed down from the bed and took two shy, padding steps toward the approaching beauty. That was when she remembered what she'd learned of Lamia, that in her own mind, at least, she was a vampire. They had discussed it and Livy said how absurd it was, that there hadn't been any vampires in centuries.

But even as her heart throbbed with excitement as she looked at Lamia, a very serious, somehow frightening doubt filled Daria's timid mind and dependent heart. Perhaps it was the incredible depth of the psychic's dark eyes; she had the impression that Lamia could be hypnotic, mesmeric, if she wished. Daria had always been the imaginative sister of the trio and there was something about their beautiful guest that reminded the petite lesbian of standing in the barren streets of a forboding western ghost town. She'd never been to one, but it wasn't hard to imagine the wind yowling and snuffling close to the ground, blowing down everything that wasn't perfectly affixed. Now Daria took a step back from Lamia. It was easy to see her as the taunting, silent shadows appearing at the swinging doors of a long-closed saloon, just a pale hand showing perhaps; a creature where any visitor knew no creatures could still exist.

Both women saw what Lamia had in her hand at precisely the same time. A candle, lit and dripping wax, like some kind of tallowed phallis urgent to be used.

Lamia did not reply to Livy. Her motions were perfectly without sound, yet deliberate and bold, fully without stealth. She did not even seem to look at them until she had discovered their quickly discarded underthings on a chair and lifted them to the candle flame.

"For God's sake, Lamia, what are you doing?" Livy demanded, throwing her long legs over the side of the bed and rising, arms akimbo. "Those are expensive things!"

Still there was no answer. Daria squealed when she saw that Lamia did not mean to singe them, but to set them afire. Already flame was leaping up from the clothes, even while Lamia continued to hold them, to make sure they were going effectively. When they had become a livid torch, Lamia moved effortlessly to the curtains and set them afire too.

She turned, then, speaking not aloud but penetratingly, even shriekingly in their heads. *The fire will be contained. I shall now allow it to spread to the rest of the house.* She smiled eerily at them, her eyes radiant with consummated joy. *It will merely be enough to burn the two of you . . . to ashes.*

"If we're going to burn, then you're coming with us!" Livy exclaimed in fury, dashing toward the lovely vampire.

"Don't, Livy!" screamed Daria. "That's only Lamia's astral projection! She isn't really here at all!"

But she was too late and Livy had grabbed at Lamia's arm, and cried out in pain and drew her hand back, tears starting in her eyes. An electrical shock had carved its way through her fingers, all the way to the shoulder; and as she looked down in agony to see the damage, she saw her hand and arm turning black, smoke rising from the useless fingers.

*You fools!* Lamia boomed in their heads, laughing joyously now, celebrantly. *You dared to challenge Lamia Zacharius and the penalty is what it has been for three thousand years: Death!*

"The door!" cried Daria, and the two of them rushed past the vampire.

But when they got there, they found not only that the door was locked from the outside but seemed to have turned to immovable, immobilized, solid smooth stone. There was no longer so much as a break or a seam all the way round the frame of the door. It was merely part of an unbroken, all enclosing wall that had become, incredibly, rock hard.

Weeping piteously and beginning to cough, Daria—with both hands—and Livy with her remaining good one, groped and pawed for an opening of any kind. A glance told them that the flame shielding the window was an impassable barrier, a wall two bare women could not breech. Their room had been universally turned to the inpenetrable substance of an ancient, quite unassailable mountain, and no exits remained.

"Please—" Livy began to beg, whirling to plead with Lamia.

But they were along. Alone, in an inferno, a raging hell just as purposive and clearly motivated as a bullet shot.

Already the flames were licking their way round the wall, edging out from them, apparently involved in a mad, chaotic race. An eating race, for already the fire was devouring a magazine rack and the periodicals in it, then rushing on to gobble hungrily at a chair. Great billows of stinking smoke filled the air, made them cough as pain lanced their lungs. Still nude, utterly vulnerable, Livy and Daria met in the center of the room, hugging one another in terror.

Then one avid length of flame, bolting like a lunatic vacuum cleaner and issuing a locomotive cloud of gusting smoke, scorched its way across the carpeting toward them, sizzling and starving, groping for their bare, shrinking toes . . .

Twenty minutes later, sensing that there was no longer a psychological obligation on her part to be asked inside because she knew that only the living, or the undead, ever offered invitations, Lamia moved down the hall and unlocked the door of the sisters' room. It swung open easily, freely, rattling against a wall.

The fire had been contained, just as she planned. That was good. Frank and Mila would only require new drapes, new carpeting, perhaps a chair or table or two—and a double funeral.

Lamia saw them in the center of the room, blackened and charred on the floor. But even at the distance from the door, she could see that they had died primarily of suffocation. Only their feet and the lower parts of their legs were actually destroyed. They looked now like four branches of an old and decaying tree. They died lying on their faces, as if seeking the last available ounce of air, and Lamia gently turned them over.

She screamed in shock and threw her hands before her face.

Flames had not reached Livy's face, or Daria's— but they were no longer the same. Their faces were parchment-like, deeply creased and cratered in the cheeks and neck. At her one sickening glance she knew they were, at least, the faces of crones more than one hundred years old. Eyes open, staring in terror and sunken in the sockets, there was some phlegmy yellow substance dripping down the craggy cheeks into the corners of their toothless mouths.

What in the name of Apollo was this? Lamia edged her way fearfully toward the door, knowing she must permit Frank and Mila to discover the dead sisters. Her own hands were trembling with shock; she couldn't quite think with her usual clarity. But the questions were rather simple, really, however difficult the answers might eventually prove to be. If these ancient crones were not Mila Triladus' sisters, *who*—and *what*—were they?

How like death-worms the wingless
  moments crawl!
The point of one white star is quivering
  still.
  —Shelley, *Prometheus Unbound*

  When night Darkens the streets
Then wander forth the sons
Of Belial, flown with insolence and
  wine . . .
  —Milton, *Paradise Lost*

# XIII

From Lamia's standpoint, the first and possibly only drawback arising from the suffocation deaths of Livy and Daria was that there was no longer any possibility of leaving for the Himalayas until after Christmas.

Just as badly, she couldn't be sure that Frank failed to suspect something more than an electrical short-circuit. Although he held her close in his arms, kissing her repeatedly on the mouth until she longed for him to quest after new locations and for more ambitious activity than kisses, the archeologist pointed out that "it would be cruel to leave Mila sisterless and on the verge of giving birth. I'm not sure she could handle it. We'll simply have to wait until the child comes and arrange for a nurse to stay with the two of them."

Lamia, at that point, was inclined to curse herself for a fool. Later, when he would be consistently working and have little time to see her, she would wonder if she hadn't left behind some telltale clue that implied—to Frank, at least—her responsibility in the twin deaths. There were even moments when she sensed that he was dissatisfied with her, possibly hurt.

They had a closed casket funeral for Daria and Livy which Frank himself arranged and at no time did he mention to Lamia the extraordinary aging of their deceased faces. She told herself that perhaps no one but the people from the mortuary had seen them, and had chosen not to alarm their brother-in-law. It was important to believe that, if she could. Otherwise, if Frank actually knew, there was some awful, grotesque secret that he shared with his dead sisters-in-law and refused to share with her. If he were waiting for her to broach the subject in order to accuse her, her beloved Frank would have to wait until he was at least as old as she. In this December-May relationship, the old age turnabout was reversed and Lamia never intended for her young potential lover to learn the truth.

Lamia felt somewhat better when it occurred to her, quite reasonably, that the scientist might have been as amazed by the sister's appearance of extreme age as she was, but kept quiet in order to avoid any chance of Mila finding out. With his education, he had to know that such a shock, now, might abort the child and Lamia wished there was some way to let Mila know. Whatever the truth might be, there was something *Dorian Gray-like* to the whole ghastly mess and she was delighted when Livy and Daria were six feet underground with a ton of dirt on their chests.

Coming back to the mortuary limousine in a light snowfall, climbing a slightly frozen slope to the berm of the road, Lamia observed with surprise that Frank appeared to be grieving more for the young women's loss than Mila herself. Or, at any rate, he showed the losses more clearly. She pretended to lose her footing for a moment, trying both to avoid a confrontation with Mila and the shuddery Greek Orthodox bearded minister trailing after her. Why was it, she wondered, that the older religions tended to have such solemn, authoritative representatives? The old fellow looked like actors Nehemiah Persoff and Jack Kruschen, sharing the role of Moses. Here, she mused, this aged part of the cemetery seemed almost deserted. It would not have been hard to believe that Pythagoras or Vrukalakos once paid somebody to keep it ready for their midnight digs. Weeds leaped like wounded secrets from the gravelly edge of the road and the laconic black gravediggers gave the impression that they'd finish filling in the sister's graves by Easter. When she saw the aging minister was on her heels, his passionate eyes boring into the back of her head, Lamia scrambled up the hill to the limousine.

They drove back across U.S. Forty and Lamia realized that Thessaly waited, several miles out. Of course, no one was being permitted to get within six or seven miles of her beloved town these days. Police and the National Guard had the road blocked off; locating and killing the monster Aether had been foremost on the authorities' collective minds since little Eddie reported the killing of his parents. Soon, she sensed, disturbed by the silence in the mortuary vehicle and the way Frank simply peered out the curtained window, Aether would tire of being hunted and become—at the second he wished it—the hunter. How far his attacks would range before she and Frank reached Asia and persuaded Demogorgon to return with them was anybody's guess.

Soon it was December and the small, well-kept

180

streets of Lawrence handled an increasing amount of traffic. The Triladus' neighbors seems to be constantly on the go, Christmas shopping. Eventually Frank relented despite Mila's growing sense of loneliness and brought an immense, artificial tree home with him. Mila listlessly threw several handfuls of icicles and "snow" onto the green branches. watching as Frank and Lamia handled the bigger portion of the task. In the background, an old record of Bing Crosby singing *White Christmas* continued sticking—always after the words "to hear . . . sleighbells in the snow"—and Mila was always slow to rise and prod the stereo's stubborn arm. It was already vaguely weird, nightmarish, when Frank said in low tones to anyone who cared to listen: "Somehow I think it's appropriate that we have an artificial tree. A phony tree. Anything genuine from nature would wither the moment we brought it into the house."

That was when Frank began spending most of his time working alone in his laboratory or at the University, always greeting Lamia with a secret hug or kiss but obviously feeling that he no longer required her efforts. She'd already revealed every secret possible from his ancient chest of Triladus memories, and she had the impression that he might have no further use of her until they actually caught a plane for the Himalayas. That made matters worse; his obvious male chauvinism. Lamia wanted badly to point out that he

181

wouldn't even know where he was going without her psychometric gifts.

But it also made her eager for Mila to have the child and get it over with. Her impatience expanded apace with the tall woman's swollen belly. These days Mila seemed even more ponderous than before and, when she spoke either to her or to Frank, it was always a critical, grumbling monosyllable.

How Lamia longed to be gone with Frank Triladus. She had nothing against Mila, really, now that her grotesquely-beautiful sisters were dead. But it had been a case, for months, of Mila standing directly in her path like some sort of gargoyle redwood. She realized that first mothers were likely to be late, more so than early, but devoutly hoped Mila's delivery would prove to be an exception. She had never hungered for another man in her long life the way she craved Dr. Frank Triladus.

Although she felt reasonably certain that sex between Frank and Mila was rare, particularly in these final hazardous days of her pregnancy, it continued to give Lamia a sharp pang to watch them, on occasion, mounting the steps together. The big two-story house was chilly for someone sleeping alone and it seemed haunted now. True, Frank rarely even touched Mila and, if he did, it was so off-handedly it might have been a considerate brother displaying concern for his pregnant sister. Lamia knew that she might have become unreasonable, but she no longer had any consuming, regular duties to perform until they left and she felt increasingly isolated each time she trudged off to her bedroom by herself. Was it possible, she wondered one night when she awakened at three a.m., that she was in danger of becoming history's first spinster vampire?

After all, with Frank teaching frequent classes at Badler University as well as working in the lab, and Mila spending most of her time poking her tummy in the bedroom, Lamia's boredom could only deepen. Walking the streets of Lawrence after the sun went down, seeing the Christmas wreaths fresh and glittering in neighborhood windows and busy families placing gifts beneath trees, loneliness and boredom became a difficult, even dangerous combination in the beauteous vampire. Her imagination became more and more uncontrollable.

By Christmas Eve, with the snow spread on Lawrence ground and streets like toothpaste squeezed from a Titan's tube, Lamia found herself beginning to wonder if Frank had discovered some clue to her astral presence in the room of his sisters-in-law. Of course, he would then feel uncomfortable around her—even wary. Maybe he planned to telephone the police and, while they represented no genuine danger to her, escaping them would mean revealing her existence and another dreary manhunt, torches scorching the midnight skies, as it had been in the old days.

Perhaps too, she thought with despair, it was simply time to move on. To begin life anew somewhere else. That had always been the plight of most vampires, Lamia understood, since they either outlived ordinary people or decimated the population. She had been protected by Pythagoras and her beloved Thessalonians; but it was time to face the fact that she was no longer a special vampire, with special friends and family. She was on her own, really, and the only reason to stay— other than Frank himself—was her concern for the damage Aether would do when he finally moved into civilized streets.

But to be honest about it, what did that mean to her? Why should it matter, at all, if evil's presence ran wild in the city? What had civilization ever done for her but obstruct her, keep her in positions where she was forced to lie, stalk her kind and call them evil merely because—like many of the pathetic poor she'd seen, hungry, in nations around the world—they had a limited number of options? These civilized Americans used the poor the way a puppeteer manipulated his dummy, dragging votes from them the way a ventriloquist produced voices from his dummy's mouth. Except that the puppet himself stole from his master every chance he could get, pretending a helplessness he'd long since outgrown. The

United States had become a nation of plastic Pinocchios tripping over their ever-elongating noses and no one knew, anymore, who pulled the strings. Why should *she*, as a member of society's most despised subset—the minority group to end all minority groups and perhaps the only one without a lobby in Washington—have to feel responsible for the carnage of true evil when, at last, it came? Perhaps it was the only way man would ever grow up, would ever become "real boys!"

With no special interest in an attack and no troublesome psychological vibrations making demands upon her, Lamia chose Christmas Eve to fly on traditional batwings into the city. Perhaps there would be newly interesting matters to intrigue her, she thought. Other places which might have need of her exceptional services.

It was difficult to achieve much height in the heavy winter night but finally Lamia reached busy Keystone Avenue. The street was lined with massive shopping centers, restaurants, and motion picture theatres. She became herself again and started walking. Residents in this neighborhood were well-dressed, important-looking people and, from a glance at the crowds hustling in and out of department stores, she concluded with a smile that they were all trying to get rid of their money in one evening. On impulse, she stopped at a candy store and purchased the largest box of creams they had. Taking a gift card from the nearby table, she hesitated, then reluctantly addressed it to both Frank and Mila Triladus.

The brisk Christmas breeze reddened Lamia's cheeks as she strolled, and she felt suddenly just part of the crowd. It was a comfortable thing to do, for a change, pretending that she was only an ordinary modern young woman window shopping in a modern city. Men in Santa Claus suits jingled bells at her as she walked, looking warmer than anybody else with false beards drooping over their padded stomachs. She was thinking how horrified people would be to know that a vampire strode among them when she saw the Glendale marquee—brazen-bright over her head—and read its legend with a start. "Dracula's Honeymoon," the sign declared, and Lamia smiled before moving in close to peer at the billboards.

For many years she had known of the semi-imaginary Count Dracula. She could even remember reading the novel by Bram Stoker when it first was published. The book itself fascinated her with its collection of old myths, some of which were absolutely true and most of which were believed by villagers in the older countries. For a time she had even wondered if Stoker himself might *be* one of her kind, intentionally withholding some of the facts and twisting others for reasons of ambition and self-protection. Then, back in the thirties, she'd watched the Bela Lugosi film with a feeling

186

of rising irritation. Why would any woman be lured and enchanted by a small man in white face with a lipstick gash on his mouth? Only stupid or lazy vampires ever let themselves go that way, along with the handful of perverts like Renfield who had been unsuccessfully vampirized.

This fellow pictured on the advertisement, however, was a devilishly handsome chap. Wavy, chestnut hair; commanding eyes; good posture and the suggestion of stature and poise. Curious, Lamia fed dollar bills to the cashier, took her ticket, and went inside.

Instantly Lamia's eyes adjusted to the darkness and soon after she'd settled into a seat, her nerves began to relax. The film's atmosphere—shot in crawling shadows—seemed to appreciate the vampire's problem with strong light. Count Dracula had fallen in love, hard, with a mystery woman and Lamia nodded her approval. A man capable of love wasn't all evil. Oddly, the young woman on the screen didn't look a great deal different than herself. In an eerie way, it was like seeing herself on the—

A hand was in her lap.

It belonged to a bleary-eyed, out-of-shape man with a pencil-stroke of a moustache. Looking up, startled, she saw his anxious experimental smile. In a flash, Lamia knew that the man was an accountant at a large department store in charge of late payments; a soldier who'd served in

Vietnam; a member of a fraternal organization, either the Shrine or the Knights of Columbus; a moderate Democrat who got misty when the flag passed in review; a dutiful son (one of three children), and the married father of a boy and a girl. He had a few thousand dollars in the bank, he always went to church at Easter, and he liked clam chowder from *Arthur Treacher's Fish & Chips* and Whoppers from *Burger King*, and he honestly believed that he loved his wife.

Wanting no trouble, Lamia took the man's hand, lifted it away. It came back quickly, feeling her breast this time. His breath was steamy on her face. She sighed and looked around the theatre. No more than half-a-dozen people were there, presumably because the timing of the film's release on Christmas Eve left something to be desired. The others were several rows away, engrossed in the movie or in each other. Lamia looked back at the man and said, "Please." His smile widened; his fingers pinched and they hurt. She had the notion that he thought of his groping hand as something apart from himself, something over which, now and then, he had little control.

Lamia smiled back. Radiantly. Then she leaned across the arm of the chair, gave the man a light kiss on the mouth, and ducked her head in the hollow between his head and shoulder. His first sound was one of delighted amazement. Lamia rested her own arm across the upper part of his

188

legs, holding him down, and casually cupped his mouth with the palm of her other hand.

His last sound was muffled, scarcely enough to disturb anyone else in the theatre. His legs thrashed uselessly against her pinning arm. The hands that had pawed and mauled sought to push her away, and failed. Lamia's fanged incisors cut deep into his throat. She angled her mouth so that she could chew diagonally, toward the jugular, and found it. Getting purchase, the teeth sunk into the cord of life, she bit all the way through, and pulled her head back.

Practice makes perfect and Lamia knew how to accept the blood without getting a spot on her clothing. When the stranger's head fell forward on his chest, she released his mouth and heard a distinct "whoof" marking his final breath.

After several more minutes passed, Lamia arose and walked up the aisle to the lobby. Locating a manager, she touched his arm lightly to get his attention. "You have a masher on the far right, twelfth row up," she said, scarcely breaking her stride.

"I'll take care of him," the manager said with a sigh as she headed for the street.

"Don't rush," she called coldly, over her shoulder. "There's no hurry at all."

Winging her way back to the Triladus house, Lamia's anger began to supplant her loneliness. She felt genuinely outraged by her contacts with the outer world. What were human beings coming to when a respectable woman couldn't walk on Indianapolis' main artery or see a motion picture without being attacked? Why wasn't anyone doing anything about the real crimes of the city?

Trembling with indignation, she let herself into her room and decided that she had another crusade to interest her, in case the relationship with Frank fell apart. She would become the first vampire vigilante.

But it was all just idle diversion and, before she could fall asleep, the lonely tears again filled her eyes. If only things would work out with the archeologist, she'd ask for nothing more in this strange world. Unless, of course, it was that suave and charming man who'd played Count Dracula. Why, he made a girl want to go right back to the beginning and lose her humanity all over again!

She seem'd, at once, some penanced
    lady elf,
Some demon's mistress, or the demon's
    self.
               —Keats, *Lamia*


We are the ministers of pain, and fear,
And disappointment, and mistrust,
    and hate . . .
        —Shelley, *Prometheus Unbound*


# XIV


Dogs, horses, cats rarely have psychosomatic symptoms of illness—which is to say that they are seldom neurotic—and persist in having a good time from life until the moment they die. That shows how ignorant they are, because they do not know they will perish.

Man, on the other hand, finds such stark signposts as the ages thirty, forty, sixty and sixty-five a source of half-imagined illness because he recognizes the fact that he must die someday. Supreme among animals in his knowledge, he often quits most of the things that brought him happiness and sits down to wait for death. If it takes another twenty years, thirty-five or fifty years, eventually he manages to prove that he was right about dying all along. That shows how intelligent man is.

When gigantic Aether, the Titan, returned to the Vale of Aphaca and descended to the bottom-most level of Antipodes to plan his course of action, he was neither quite an animal nor quite a man. As first days and then weeks passed. While human beings above him on the surface oohed and ahhed at the terrible deaths of the decent Pike family, Aether was, at best, vaguely aware of time going by. Like houseflies who cram a lot into twenty-four hours, Aether was on his own clock. It didn't matter to him that people were creating roadblocks, loading rifles, summoning experts in the art of dealing death. Because he knew, secondhand, what death was but really never expected to experience it.

In that and other senses, Aether could be viewed as earth's first terrorist. If he had been more intelligent and better able to reason the way humans do, he might have begun the first terrorist organization and cost the entire world its life. Such a being has an entirely different outlook on death than either the lower animals or humankind, and consequently a different view on life and its significance. If one did not have to experience death nor its preparatory sisters, pain and disease, and cared for no one who *did* die, a certain bloodless detachment sets in. A detachment which lies at the muddy, cold heart of all brutality, all murder. If he had been able to reason he might have said that the way to stop terrorism was to make its exponents realize they could be hurt, could be killed and would achieve nothing whatever in the process.

Slaying people did not, as a consequence of Aether's condition, seem particularly dreadful to Aether. Dying the way he inflicted it didn't take long. Dead victims felt nothing at all when they were eaten. They could scarcely miss themselves, when they were gone, since an afterlife rarely occurred to the dragon. And since he'd never felt for another being of any kind, he was incapable of grasping the fact that other people *did* long for those who were taken from life. In kind with most human beings, in any case, Aether hadn't ever planned to be evil, it just happened that way. It was his stamp of individuality, it was what he did. He saw it as a natural outcropping of living in a world which detested him on sight. Since those who saw him ran away screaming and cared nothing for him or his avid feelings, there was no reason to care about anybody else. If he appeared alien to them, they were more so to him. It wasn't, for Aether, a case of doing evil things or even the matter of an eye-for-an-eye. It was a straight forward matter of occasionally needing to dine, and preferring, of all the ghastly things he'd eaten, the flesh of living man and woman.

Once the vampire-servant Vrukalakos had grown talkative and tried to explain it all to him. Aether had thought, rather grumpily, how he didn't understand the distinction between human people eating cattle and his eating human people. That's what everybody was there for. The cattle never seemed to mind. Cows had never sent out for guns or bombs in order to avoid the broken neck at the slaughterhouse. They had a certain commendable docility, a sense of the fitness of things which Aether admired, and he hoped that if he ever encountered anyone or anything capable of shattering his own spine, he'd be as level headed about it as your typical cow or sheep.

But now it was time to ascend to the surface again and put his plan into practice. Aether had a fresh, huge appetite. His plan was to work and eat his way straight across the nation to the west, swing north to the border, hang a right and keep going until he got to New York. He'd heard about New York once and thought it might be his kind of place.

It would be marvelous to leave Antipodes for good. Bad things needed room to expand and they tired quickly of sycophants and slaves. For centuries he'd had a work force of his own to tend to his needs here, at the center of the earth, but the repulsive creatures were getting on his nerves. Sometimes the pain they carried with them every step reached a surface of their own, exploding into shrieking sounds of agony. Then, too, they were so indescribably ugly to Aether that he'd always despised looking at them. Not so much the human people he'd revivified in order to maintain them as slaves for eternity, but the actual demons which evil had devised. Most of them tripped on things when they lurched around the cave floor, especially those creatures with knuckles that swept the floor from mishapen arms. The squalid things with the scaly bodies simply stank worse than Aether did, and the beings formed in the shape of articles of human anatomy hardly carried their own weight. Rolling heads, scrabbling fingers, slipsliding buttocks could scarcely get around any more.

Leaving them to fend for themselves and do without his guidance, Aether began dragging himself hungrily up the rocky tunnel to the waiting world outside. He used his numerous clawed appendages to propel him forward, balancing with the great tail. He remembered overhearing Pythagoras' rather flattering description of him when the impossibly ancient mathematician and philosopher was only yards from here, explaining things to Mary Graham. She asked him what Aether was and the old man replied: "Once it was said that his name was a symbol for the essential breath of man, the spirit-presenting gift of animation, vivification. Now I have come to know that Aether is much more than that, something that existed long before my people and I, before prehistoric man and before the great reptiles trod the jungle floor. Something that might have been produced from a frown of God, or a smile of Satan, millenia ago." Aether had especially liked Pythagoras' final comment: "I think it is a horrid clue to what lies near the heart of all life and to the dismal need of death."

In its malevolent way, the monstrous beast smiled in the darkness of his climbing tunnel. That aged fellow had been a genius, no question of that. Because the truth of the matter was that, until Aether came to earth, *no creature had ever died. Because no creature had known it must, had never believed it about himself or any other. Not knowing it at all, no creature attacked another or gave sorrow or pain. It was a matter of deep pride to enormous Aether that he, alone, the walking eternal symbol of everything bad and wrong with life, had brought death to the planet Earth. Creatures remembered the terrible obligation of death as they evolved. The message was telegraphed along the veins and whispered in the subtly-altering genes, the first communique conveyed as though by awful instinct. And after thousands of years, and thou-*

*sands of adapting evolutions, the message finally reached the soft, pink new ears of the being called Human: I am born to die.*

It was the very first thing man or woman ever believed. Deities came afterward, along with viciousness and carnality, and the neatness of it, of course, was that it was also the *last*.

Always.

He crawled eagerly out into the Vale of Aphaca and, that moment, he blinked when the searing flashes of light from gun muzzles flicked at him. Some of them struck, but he didn't know it.

Aether stared in wonderment at the tableau before him, his demeanor that of an aging businessman surprised by a dinner table set for a party. His giant's mouth fell open in delight. He'd never seen so many people together at one time and, best of all, they were all living! He wriggled his immense butt in the dirt with joy, feeling like a small boy given a free pass to a *Baskin & Robbins*.

After the initial explosions were seen for a passing nuisance and a time lapsed to adjust to the continual irksome flash of bullets passing his eyes, Aether waded into them, his countless clawing hands reaching like a child collecting leaves for a biology scrapbook. His massive feet stepped, grindingly, while he tried to remember not to mash them into inedible jelly. His movements were deft, surprising for his size. From the standpoint of the policemen and

National Guardsmen, it was much more than surprising, it was utterly devastating. Off guard, his step became the cause of death or, just as badly, being pinned by his cruel hands against the stinking, spined side of his titanic body. Once there they wriggled and seeped blood like bugs on a board.

Ah, the screaming! Beaming, trying to see and hear everything at once, Aether crunched and crunched again. They were infinitely better than carrion, Vrukalakos' miserable offerings. This flesh was hot, tasty, fresh; what the vampire brought him was stale many days or months before he arrived, and Aether saw that the vampire had appealed to his vanity, his love of service.

But at one point in the annihilation he so gleefully wrought Aether paused as a rare memory occurred to him: Vrukalakos once had a friend! A woman vampire named Lamia. She was the most beautiful creature Aether had ever seen and she hadn't accompanied the silly suicidal folk of Thessaly when they marched into his tunnel. Aether remembered, now, how he had longed to possess her as a preliminary to devouring her. Perhaps, he thought with a twinge of mingled desire and loneliness, again dipping his long neck to nip off a helmeted head, perhaps she was somewhere nearby even now. Perhaps he could find Lamia Zacharius and make his joy complete.

\*　　　\*　　　\*

When Lamia was next awakened in bed, it was still the night of Christmas Eve and, instead of nightmares or lesbians, she found Frank Triladus sitting beside her. His eyes were disquieting, a mixture of longing for her and some dreadful matter on his mind.

But Lamia misunderstood, throwing off the covers and drawing him down to her. She held him against her naked body, showering his face with kisses, and for awhile he did not protest. Instead, for the first time, he responded totally and allowed his hands to roam over her breasts and downward to cup her buttocks against his pajamaed form. "Get out of those things quickly," she whispered against his cheek, nearly chattering with excitement. "You're vastly overdressed for the occasion."

Although she had felt his maleness throbbing and pressing against her, he again tore himself away. Pushing himself to a seated position, gasping for breath, he took her hand and squeezed it until it hurt. "My lovely, desirable Lamia, now is not the time. Soon, though, in the Himalayas—sooner than you think!"

What he had added dispelled her initial sense of loss. "The baby . . . ?"

His chin bobbed. "It's coming," he said "right now!"

"Where's the doctor?"

"Don't you remember, Mila never wanted one." He tugged her to her bare feet, scarcely able to keep his eyes and hands off her. "I'll know what to do, I think. Please, hurry—you have to assist me!"

Her eyes were huge and dark with wonder. "I've never tried to—to bring life into the world."

Frank held her in his arms and she saw, suddenly, how frightened and young he looked. "Don't desert me now, Lamia, darling. I need your help."

"Of course," she said simply, spinning and reaching for her robe.

They began hurrying down the shadowed hallway leading to Mila's bedroom and, after a few yards, she heard the awful sounds reaching out for them. For a moment Lamia thought Aether was there, but they were only the cries of a woman deep in the throes of labor. Man of science and ancient vampire looked at each other, scared. When they reached her room, the door was wide open and light leaped from it across the corridor. In surprise, Lamia gasped. Again Frank Triladus' shadow, cast on the opposite wall, was towering, enormous. Then he was half-dragging her after him into the bedroom.

Lamia smiled. They were doing something together again—he needed her! Lamia's heart soared with shivers of joy. Together! Perhaps, even now, there was a way to let the unifying newborn die . . .

All spirits are enslaved which serve
    things evil.
            —Shelley, *Prometheus Unbound*

## XV

Although Lamia scurried around the aging two-story house to bring lamps from other rooms in an effort to make their task somewhat more visible, it remained a darkened make-shift operating theatre and Mila's bloodcurdling shrieks quickly got on the vampire's normally shockproof nerves. The enormous mother-to-be had a way of lolling off into a somnolent stage, her rising belly like that of a whale about to surface, then suddenly wildly staring about her as screams of fright, pain and possibly other torments poured from her mouth.

It was hard not to be jealous of the solicitious Frank Triladus, sweating profusely above the big woman in the bed. His duties were mostly a question of shifting and replacing towels, of daubing at Mila's perspiring forehead with a wash cloth; but his concern was clearly genuine. Lamia was surprised by the gentleness he displayed and somewhat dismayed by the jealous way he protected Mila. When she approached the bed, she saw the archeologist's stern gaze attentive upon her. He could not possibly know how she longed for Mila to lose this child, the one thing that might restore their relationship. Nor could he know that, while Lamia observed the incredible process of birth—of life entering the world, rather than leaving it—she abandoned all intention of harming the infant.

As a matter of fact, while Lamia watched the time-honored miracle and saw two tiny feet begin to emerge from a female on the precise wave of breech-devised motherhood, she was truly touched. Touched in only a way a woman who has never given birth can be, in a wistful, why-didn't-I-think-of-that? kind of fashion that produced a vast sense of emptiness, even loss. It had never occurred to Lamia before that there might be something fulfilling—a different variety of immortality, perhaps—about having a child. She had rarely even cared to form close relationships with men and only Frank himself had roused in her an urge for permanency with the opposite sex. To hear the way Frank whispered encouragingly to Mila, "Push! Harder now, that's the girl—that's the girl—another push now!" and watch the precarious journey of the rather courageous child down the birth canal was yet another startling revelation for Lamia Zacharius in a year of self-discovery.

She jumped and looked around. It seemed to be getting colder in the room. Outside the house winter winds were howling furiously and gusts of wind continually rattled against the panes, like *things* trying to get in. She shook off the feeling and wondered if her awe might be involved with the fact that this was Christmas Eve, reminiscent of another lonely scene when she was young. There would be no trio of wise men journeying from afar to witness the arrival of this child. If there was, they would freeze to death before they made it. Yet there remained something valiant, something of the eternal, about the birth. Mila was in a house thousands of miles from her native land, delivering a baby with the awkward aid of her husband instead of getting the professional care available in any well-appointed, modern hospital.

Yes, she nodded. Something of the—eternal.

Suddenly, considerable doubt—and a key question—filled Lamia's intelligent mind. It had occurred to her that what was happening did not, if you stopped to think about it, make a great deal of sense. Did it really add up for Mila to take such risks as this simply because she was old-fashioned and was born in another country? Didn't modern Greek women seek the best, the safest possible care in having children, just like their American cousins? What conceivable point could be proven this way? When it came down to it, exactly why had Mila insisted on seeing no physicians throughout her entire pregnancy and decided to have her child at home?

Heartbeat accelerating, she looked at Frank, starting to broach the subject to him and then changing her mind. Just suppose, she mused, for the sake of argument, just suppose that Mila had some deeply private reason of her own for doing things this way. Just suppose she was concealing something, something horrible. Something that had to do, perhaps, with—with what? She shook her head. Because the only thing she could imagine that Mila might be concealing was the infant itself.

Moving whirls of windblown snow began spreading in clever designs on the other side of the window glass, like pale, anemic blood being patterned by some lunatic artist. Lamia shivered and held her arms with her hands. It was getting colder in the room, now, she was sure of it. It was almost as if someone had slipped into the dark cellar and turned off the ancient furnace, causing not only the freezing temperatures of this room but a new, secret silence. She risked another glimpse of Frank Triladus and realized something else that wasn't right, wasn't right at all. While

204

Frank was certainly being exceptionally cautious and doing his level best for Mila, there was yet something . . . lacking . . . in his approach. For a moment, it eluded her; then she had it. He wasn't excited about the baby coming.

And he never had been, not for a moment. His actions, during the preceding nine months and now weren't those of any first father she'd ever seen. There was a cold part of the man that remained detached, observant, even wary. Gentle and thorough, yes: but not involved. And surely not upset, not even now.

When Lamia caught sight of the thin coating of blood smearing the gradually-emerging child and sensed the peculiarly hard-to-define not-rightness of what was happening, it would not have surprised her to hear, above the old house, a chorus of angels singing. A chorus of darkly demonic angels, their sacred, mumbled Latin hiding mad curses, dire imprecations, and hideous promises. If three wise men rapped on the door now, they would have horns.

She was being silly! Startled, then, by her own shift of mood from near reverence to ominous expectation, Lamia made herself peer again at Mila. Her feminine heart shared the big woman's common misery. The anguish of her distorted, pale face and the writhing of her thrashing, enormous limbs renewed the tender interest she had initially felt.

"C-Can I help?" she whispered, plaintive beside Frank.

He grunted, his hands held like a quarterback accepting a snap from center. "Help me catch it when it comes all the way out," he replied without looking at her, "because this kid is heavy as hell! Don't worry, I'll cut the cord." Suddenly he laughed, inclining his head as the fat infant buttocks popped into sight. "Look there, Lamia, look! It's a boy. A great, big, powerful little boy! How marvelous for Mila!"

But something was wrong. She sensed it when she got her glimpse of the baby's body, something was not right. Did newborns customarily have so much hair? It was hard to see clearly in the gloom of Mila's bedroom and she positioned herself rapidly, draped in white towels at the new mother's naked feet.

"Here come the shoulders." It was an ordinary enough announcement yet she had heard a subtle change in Frank's voice. A note of doubt had crept in, in accompaniment with what he was seeing. "And—*here comes the head!*"

She caught a fleeting glimpse of hair at the instant of his rasping cry, and then he was moving, instantly, shielding the child with his big body—shielding it so that Lamia could not see. "Oh dear Father," he mumbled, scarcely above a whisper. "Sweet Apollo, she's gone and done it!" He glanced briefly behind him at Lamia, his face a twisted mask of fierceness and of fright. Warning, too, was there as he cried his strangled plea: "For God's sake, Lamia don't look!"

But she saw the awkward way he was gripping the infant and, with her heart thundering, Lamia craned her neck to see. And for the rest of her life she would wish she hadn't.

Dizzied, stepping back, Lamia heard the dark, demonic chorus crescent, the triumphal clamor reverberating against the walls of the bedroom in a thousand manic discords. Unable to stop, she went on staring—staring at that which had finally emerged from the new mother on the blood-soaked bed.

Mila's newborn was of the breed which came out at night to swarm in the family house like killer bees, ripping things asunder. Sometimes, when it was larger, it feasted on members of its own family. The very worst of its kind could kill with a look—but that took practice.

The swollen infant laying half in Frank's quivering arms and half on the bed between its weakened mother's sprawled white legs, seemed simultaneously black and white. It depended upon the splotches of angry skin one saw first. Its head was simply enormous, with squinting bloodshot eyes already open and staring. Hair the color of week-old snow sprung from its scalp and dripped down the whole length of its grotesque body. Hair, too, grew like black wire from his flared nostrils and in its brow and from a spot between the shoulder blades. A full set of small, pointed teeth flickered when it opened its carmine lips. Its biceps, Dos Kodion, Lamia thought, its biceps were nearly as big around as Frank's and the dangling arms extended all the way down. Its sausage fingers were playing, picking, playing, picking at obese toes with nails two inches long. The cord of life still connected with its mother looked like something alive unto itself; it was thick as hemp and throbbed with blood still coursing and caking from the supine woman.

Mila had given birth to a living goblin. A loathsome creature about whom others had only dared to whisper in the past, with baleful terror lurking in their hearts. Frank suddenly found his nerve and, with a carving knife, severed the cord with a sound like snapping bone. When he put the creature over his shoulder to slap it into life, it growled at him and something yellow-green with curds like Quaker oats fouled his back and left smouldering holes in his shirt.

Mila had given birth to a *Kallikantzaros*.

Lamia turned her head anxiously to the mother, hoping she had not seen it. Perhaps something could be . . . *done* with it . . . before the woman caught sight of the thing. But Mila was half out of bed, staring, a beatific smile moving on her lips. An expression that might have been almost divine, but distinctly was not, wreathed her entire small face.

Only Lamia heard her whisper, "Thank God it's all right."

There thou art, and dost hang, a
    writhing shade,
'Mid whirlwind-peopled mountains;
    all the gods
Are there, and all the powers of name-
    less worlds,
Vast, sceptred phantoms; heroes, men,
    and beasts;
And *Demogorgon*, a tremendous
    gloom.
        —Shelley, *Prometheus Unbound*

# XVI

Lamia had wanted to stay until the wee hours, after mother and child were asleep, asking questions and hoping Frank had some of the answers. First he replied laconically with a question: "Surely you don't want to go to a late mass?" Then, realizing he'd been rude, he kissed her and said that he was both too shocked and too exhausted to talk about it. With nowhere else to go, Lamia had propped a dresser and chair against her bedroom door for the first time in her long life.

In the morning, she might have said she didn't sleep a wink, considering how weary and jittery she found herself, except there was no way to deny the sequence of diabolical nightmares which stole good rest from her. All them, without exception, involved Mila's baby boy. If, indeed, anything so revolting and half-human could be termed either a baby or a boy. She had seen him in her dreams standing outside the house, with the rooftop at his diapered waist, drooling down the chimney. She had seen him picking up insects to eat and breaking the legs of furry kittens.

What had capped going to bed the previous, terrible night before was the distinct impression she'd had that even while she was reluctantly tucking a soft blue blanket around the creature, her hands trembling, the child was already growing. Watching him steadily would have been like observing time-lapse photography, Lamia thought; and nothing in the world could ever have made her watch it that long.

Arising early, as usual, Lamia spent three minutes in the bathroom, dressed, then rushed past Mila's bedroom door and down the steps to the kitchen. She had felt empty, in a rather nauseous way. But standing before the cold refrigerator door only reminded her of Mila's freezing room during the birth and she settled for a large tomato juice, then wandered off toward the Triladus laboratory.

As she opened the door light rushed out at her from Frank's wide picture window and everything about the lab looked at once colorless and eye-achingly glaring. She saw the monstrous incongruity of his expensive, artificial Christmas tree and shuddered. Shielding her eyes with her hand, shaking a little, she went inside to close the drapes. Another Christmas morning, the anniversary of certain dreadful events at Thessaly a year ago when another child of hell was venerated. If there had been a package under the three the length of Mila's newborn, she would never have opened it. But there were no gifts at all beneath the tree and she took two more hesitant steps into the laboratory.

"I have one, last test for you, my darling."

Lamia jumped, whirled. It was her Frank, wearing a bathrobe over his pajamas and sitting slumped in a chair at the far end of the metallic table. He was motionless, unwilling to move, and he had something of cloth in his lap. The sun was in her eyes and she couldn't identify it. She went to him at once, happy when he raised his lips for her to kiss them. Instinctively, needfully, Lamia put her arms round his heavy neck and held the kiss for long seconds. "Oh, Frank, how very odd life has become lately! I couldn't even survive this strange world if it wasn't for you."

He watched her brush a black wave from her forehead and straighten his arms covering the cloth-object in his lap. "Oh, I think you'd make it without me," he said slowly, smiling. "Of all the people I've known in a long life, my Lamia, you're the born survivor of the lot. You'll be here after the rest of us are dust."

"Don't be silly." She'd turned, located a chair near the artificial tree. She tapped her fingers nervously on the arm of the chair, concerned by his proximity to the truth. "I just do what a girl must do—"

"To survive. Exactly." He laughed rather humorlessly and then sat straight in his own chair, the tangled dark hair of his chest showing above the last pajama button. "I suppose you're full of questions?"

"How is Mila? And the—the baby?"

He shrugged, averting her gaze. "So far as I know, mother and child are doing as well as can be expected. But never mind them." He sighed heavily. Looking back to her, his eyes were large, luminous with anticipation. "If things turn out well today, my darling, we'll soon fly away from this madness. We'll be together at last, the way we both want our lives to be."

"Wonderful!" But she'd heard the dubious tone of his voice. "When can we fly to Asia?"

"When the two of us become honest with one

213

another," he said steadily, and rose. The bundle of cloth seemed heavy in his arms. It filled them. "If we cannot speak the truth after all this time, we should not be together. And then there would be no flight to Asia or to the Himalayas. You see, your psychometric skills have already provided me with the personal information I sought. I know, now, that the objects in the chest were not only from my own family, but belonged to a single man." He walked slowly toward her, his face flushed. "I've had to face the facts at last and so must you."

"I don't understand." She pressed her back against the chair. "I have no idea what you're t-talking about."

"Ah, but I believe you know quite well what I mean," he corrected her, looking down at the lovely vampire. "Perhaps the last test I mentioned when you entered the laboratory will start us on the path to veracity." His breath, even from where he stood over her, was hot on her forehead and cheeks.. "Here! Tell me what your psychometric powers inform you about the man who wore this!"

With one quick gesture, Frank Triladus spread the cloth, jerked it out in front of Lamia who saw, at once, that it was a great, spreading cloak, formed like the coat of many colors owned by the Biblical Joseph.

And it was the largest, most voluminous coat

214

she had ever seen. Lamia gaped at it in amazement and finally reached forward to touch it with sensitive fingers. The slightest feel was immediately electric, charged with a galaxy of meanings for her. But she ignored them, just then, more curious about the cloak itself than she was its owner.

"Almighty Apollo, Frank," she gasped, "if this is a genuine cloak, or coat, then the man who owned it was immense! Gigantic!" Her head had to turn to take it all in. She saw that it could have been used as a blanket for a double bed and had considerable material left over. "Its wearer would have to be, why, twenty or twenty-five feet tall and weigh more than a thousand pounds!"

Frank's smile was faint, even hesitant. "At least," he amended. "But what do you make of its vibrations, psychometrically? What can you pick up from the past of this ancient garment?"

Lamia paused, then cuddled great folds of the coat in her lap, holding the sleeves first against her cheeks and then between her breasts. For a moment, although positively charged with electromagnetic memories, the impulses coming to her were confused, like a hundred telegraphic messages dot-dashing from every direction of the compass. Its owner had been everywhere, lived dozens of different ways. Holding the garment was like getting a grip on history.

Then, as her nerves calmed and she began to

control and discipline her uncanny skills, the information assuming form in Lamia's mind was clear and getting clearer. "It was worn by a man, indeed, a living man. Over two thousand years ago, I believe," she continued, her voice husky and so low she might have been communicating only with herself or those beyond the veil, "for purposes connected with his—his domain. This man was a tremendous leader, as impressive as his size. But he did not always need to be so enormous, he could alter his dimensions when he wanted to." Her eyes flicked toward him, saw how silently, how soberly, he waited. "Why, Frank, this is all so . . . peculiar. Yet I f-feel it is the truth. I'm not making this up."

He touched her cheek tenderly. "Go on, dear Lamia." His eyes were hungry. "Please proceed."

She closed her eyes for a deeper psychic interpretation and swirling motes of long-dead time came tumbling into her special vision. "There were those who said that this man was—was evil, a terrible creature who did terrible things. And—and I see that this was sometimes true. That he did do many dreadful things involving killing and slavery. And—and horrid superstitious beliefs in which numerous persons actually worshipped him. But he did what he thought was necessary and he was as full of contradictions as any normal man." She whisked a fold of cloth before her sensual lips. "Those whom he loved—his family, for example and some woman, a woman whom he positively cherished—occasionally saw his kindness, even his urge to protect."

Then she stopped and looked up, an expression of astonishment on her features.

The archeologist hesitated before speaking. When he did, it was in low, confidential tones. "There's more, Lamia, isn't there? You feel something else, don't you? Tell me, please. Tell me whatever else you feel?"

Lamia's gaze strayed to the window. Beyond this room the snow still fell, heavy now, as silent and stealthy as death waiting for the unwary on a lightless nocturnal highway. She dropped the huge cloak to the floor and folded her hands together to keep them from shaking. "This man is . . . alive, Frank. The owner of this great, immense garment is still alive!"

He gave her a simple nod and let the realization wash over her before speaking. Then he took Lamia into his arms and held her close to him. He sensed her trying to pull loose but held on. "The coat is mine, Lamia, just as you suspect this moment. I have suffered many lapses of memory over the decades and centuries. I'm sure a psychologist would say I was only trying unconsciously to deny my past, the horrible things I did when I was young, two thousand years ago. I placed the classified ad because it was time to face

217

the truth, and because of all the things I had managed to forget, I *never* once forgot you." He kissed her cheek tenderly. "Yes, always in the back of my mind I knew that once, somewhere in lost time, I had known a perfect beauty, a perfect intellect, whom I could love. When I lost her, when I was derided by my own countrymen who dared to speak my name, my family and I began to wander. My sisters accompanied me just the way that good Greek women have always followed their menfolk."

"Your . . . sisters?"

He nodded soberly. "All three of them, Lamia. Livy, and Daria, and Mila. No, do not fear me because you had to slay two of them." He sighed. "There was something about our travels throughout the world—some modern impurity of the air, or perhaps the water—that ruined them, one by one. First Livy, then Daria, whom Livy herself perverted."

"Then M-Mila is not your wife, your woman?"

"Never. Only my sister, my last living kinsman. Our size is our only familial similarity. Lamia, I swear to you that that thing she gave birth to upstairs is *not* my child. I only assisted in bringing it into the world because she craved it so badly."

"But w-what is a *Kallikantzaros*, really?" she whispered in his ear. "And . . . who is its father?"

He did not answer at once. "There was a time

when you saw my younger sisters sleeping in their bedroom. I know that you observed the lurid pentagram they had scrawled on the floor in chalk. Other times, perhaps, you heard them crooning to it, praying, Zeus help them, to the lords of the underworld. I fear they were assisting Mila in bringing . . . something unbearably monstrous, malformed and evil . . . to her lonely spinster's bed. A demonic creature of Hades, a lieutenant there, I understand. Modern people do not realize they have more than Satan or his evil child to fear. Hades is filled with dark spirits who are eager to feed on the contemporary weaknesses, the madness, of this world."

"How awful," Lamia said softly against his face.

"That monster Mila birthed," he went on, "is half-human and half-ghoul." His sigh was a virtual shudder. "Mila always wanted a tiny one of her own, you know. A clever little ghoul to do her bidding. They are our people's version of the witches' familiar, when they are reared properly, obliged to do the mother's bidding. As you may have suspected, my dear, Mila isn't as dumb as she is self-involved and a little thick." He held her at arm's length to peer into her black eyes. "Except that ghouls are really far more efficient than the animals used by witches. There's almost nothing they can't do, once they put their great bulbous heads to it. And nothing they won't do."

"You asked for the truth, Frank," she said, kissing him lightly and watching him stand, moving apart from her. "You wanted us to speak the truth at last, as the final test of our union, our future together." She swallowed hard, new at making such confessions, unable to look at him then. "My darling man, I must confess to you that I am not entirely what you think—or possibly much more than that. My darling, I am a vampire. I am three thousand years old."

"I know." His voice rolled toward her, deep and authoritative. "But you had to tell me, just as I must reveal the truth to you. I have sought you everywhere, even when I no longer knew who—or what—I was. I have adored you throughout the centuries." Lamia looked up at him and saw the way his shadow from the rising flames of the fireplace loomed immense, even threatening, against the distant wall. The shadow was large enough to fit the voluminous cloak lying at Lamia Zacharius' feet. "You knew me first as . . . Demogorgon!"

Sin and Death amain,
Following *his track*, such was the will
　　of Heav'n,
Oav'd after him a broad and beat'n way
Over the *dark Abyss* . . .
　　　　　　　—Milton, *Paradise Lost*


　　Hither the sound has borne us—
　　　　to the realm
Of *Demogorgon*, and the mighty
　　　　portal,
Like a volcano's meteor-breathing
　　　chasm . . .
　　　　　　　—Shelley, *Prometheus Unbound*


## *XVII*


Lamia had begun to piece it all together even
when he knelt beside her, speaking softly of his
misplaced memories and his three faithful sisters.
But hearing him admit it shocked her. She knew
that it cost him an effort to put it all in words, to

confess his incredible roots. Yet it also sent her own mind reeling back across the boundless centuries, sent her tumbling in return to a time when she strolled on golden sands with this marvelous man in Baalbek, in Phoenicia.

Even then she had known his reputation for prowess, for might, for fantastic size. Because he had wanted to be gentle with her she had seen no more evidence of them than the fabulous city which had been built at his command. In his honor, by thousands of slaves who sometimes gave up their lives to advance the glory of a name which they did not even dare speak.

With such a violent but glorious past it was no wonder that, uncertain of his origins as he dwelled now in the mind-numbing present, Demogorgon had developed an interest in archeology. She could see him in her mind's eye, archeologist Frank Triladus, dimly spurred on to seek solutions to the past's eternal mysteries without knowing that he, himself, had been the link missing in the evolutionary history of mankind. And as he assembled his artifacts and pored over them with fascination, some certain object—this great cloak, a weapon or a tool?—had finally been . . . familiar. Slowly, then, in a gradual way that cooperated with his scientist's mind, he had found revealed to him the most shocking discovery ever encountered by a man of science. And he had chosen her to verify his findings for him—the young woman with whom he had fallen in love hundreds upon hundreds of years ago.

"I remember now," Frank said, sitting on the carpeted floor close to her, but looking at his hands, "how I tried to learn the truth even when I was aware that I was Demogorgon. My mind, even in that long-lost day and age, contained the spark of curiosity and sought the facts. I saw that despite my undisputed powers I somehow lacked the cleverness to master the world, to triumph and lead my people to world conquest. I realized that there was something lacking in me, Lamia, that something had been taken away from me when you departed." He sighed, "Your beauty, your tenderness and capacity for love, robbed me of the necessary willingness to kill whenever it was necessary. Like any common, mortal man, I no longer desired to rule as much as I desired to be ruled by one, small woman: you."

"Frank, I adored you even then, I was charmed by you and I could certainly have loved you." She spoke hastily, persuasively. "But—but they told me you were actually enormous and that your size would literally tear me apart if we ever attempted to culminate our relationship."

He didn't reply for a lengthy moment, his expression unhappy, even embarrassed. "I discovered the same facts about the person I once was, Demogorgon. And that is why, when you

223

were willing to make love to your employer, that likeable young archeologist, he refused you at the last moment. Not that he wanted to, Lamia, never that." Frank's eyes were anguished. "I only turned away from you because my research informed me that I was most likely to become Demogoron again during intercourse. Oh, excitement of other kinds might do it, too, even anger or fury. But whenever I made love in a fully satisfying way, that would be the moment when I lost all control and became monstrous in size."

She touched his hand in love and sympathy. "My poor darling." Suddenly, another thought occurred to Lamia. "But w-what about the others, before me, Frank? Surely you haven't abstained from sex for two thousand years?"

Again he looked away, frowning. "I suspect that it was such incidents as those that caused my unconscious mind's unwillingness to go on accepting its own identity. I shelved the image of Demogorgon for such a long period of time that I am not sure, anymore, precisely who I am. But as I begin talking it out with you, with the woman I love, a lot of ancient memories begin to filter into my mind." His expression was anguished, tortured. "Yes, Lamia, there were women before you, I know that now. I can still see their terrified faces in my mind's eye, even now, and I am not proud of it. Worse, I can see what they were like, after we made love." Abruptly he turned to look

224

up at her with hope. "But you see, my darling, when Mila was having her child I realized something absolutely marvelous! Lamia, you don't have to make love as yourself! We can be together?"

"What?" she asked, surprised but eager. "How?"

"D'you remember that period before Christmas when I seemed distant to you sometimes? Well, it was because I finally remembered not only who you were but what. A vampire, yes, but much more than that. You're a Greek from Thessaly who studied with Pythagoras and learned the principles of *metempsychosis!* Think of that! And last night, dearest, when we helped Mila bear that monstrous creature, I finally perceived the crucial fact." He held her hand tightly. "Lamia, you can change your form—remember? Why, you can become as large as I! Think of it, darling. You, alone, of all the women who have ever lived, may be able to accommodate me, and then we may share one another in a magnificent way never known by man or woman anywhere and anytime!"

She sat back in her chair, staring quietly at him. Clearly he might be correct, but he was becoming overwrought with his passion for her. Even as she watched, the man she'd known as Doctor Frank Triladus was growing. His robe popped away from his body and the pajama top spread down the middle, revealing his massive chest and muscular arms.

However when he knelt beside her in his new optimism for their future, Lamia saw that his size was fluctuating, not stable. Briefly he was his normal size again, then swelled to forty pounds more than his customary weight, and again reverted to normal. His hands were locked on the arms of her chair, his perspiring face inches from her. "Please, Lamia, be mine all the way. I know it's difficult this way, but you're the one who can—can benefit from my size. I'll do my level best to be the man of your dreams."

"Please, Frank, don't push it."

But he didn't seem to hear her. Instead, he was doing his best to convince her that their life together was beginning. "Do you remember, in the Bible, when Moses sent Caleb of Judah to see the land of the Phoenicins? He reported: 'We be not able to go up against the people; for they are stronger than we . . . and all the people that we saw in it are men of great stature?'"

"Yes, I guess," she agreed, nodding and worrying about his growing excitement. The collar of his pajamas frayed, then shredded. "Honey, I remember. Let's—"

"Then Caleb went on: 'And there we saw *giants*, the sons of Anak, which come of the giants; and we were in our own sight as *grasshoppers*, and so we were in their sight.'" He paused, so nervous now that he giggled over the memories cascading into his mind. Yet there was, as well, a queerly boastful streak that frigtened Lamia. "Tell me—do you begin to understand?"

She forced a smile. "Are you saying that you were all the sons of Anak?"

"I was!" He laughed proudly, foolishly. "Only me, only Demogorgon and not those who were merely my servants and slaves! Caleb exaggerated to keep from going back, that's all. You must realize, Lamia, that the acropolis and other monuments of the period still mystify experts this very day. Oh, scientists don't talk about them much, because there are no explanations—none that they can understand—and it embarrasses them to be fooled by a past more than three hundred years before Christ!"

"I see," Lamia said slowly. "If contemporary experts can't figure out how those marvels can exist, poor old Caleb and his people really had no chance at all to understand it."

"Right, right!" He bobbed his big head. When he simply doubled his fist with enthusiasm, the sleeve of his pajama top split and dangled over his wrist. "Consider the surprise Caleb had when he stared at doorways twenty feet high! The door mortal was obliged to see the way that each of my great stones increased with size, as my buildings soared toward the sky, sometimes reaching individual widths of sixty-four feet, thirteen feet

227

in height and ten feet thick!" He laughed, and squeezed her hand. It hurt. "Lamia, each block weighed one thousand tons! Think of the way the ancient mystery deepens, even today! D'you realize that no group of puny men could possibly lift such blocks into place, higher and higher. Not then, Lamia, and not today! But there they are!"

She licked her lips thoughtfully, still humoring him. "How did such great blocks get where they are?"

But Frank didn't seem to hear her. "There are no cranes made capable of coping with such stones and monoliths, darling. Our largest modern crane lifts four hundred tons, so it would take three of them simply to hoist one solid Baalbek stone!" He giggled again. "And old Caleb saw them there, puzzled like the experts of today. And after he actually saw me, he could only conclude that all of us were a race of giants!" He stood, each pants leg splitting along the sides. Thighs and calves larger than waists popped into sight. "And all this time, sweet Lamia, eternal love, there was but one Demogorgon—one. Me!" Now he was at least seven feet tall, then quickly six-nine, then perhaps seven-one, as his size continued to alter before her gaze. "*I* built those structures, Lamia. *I* was the one who raised the stones into place. And *I did it with my bare hands!*"

Heap on thy soul, by virtue of this
    Curse,
Ill deeds, then be thou damned,
    beholding good . . .
        —Shelley, *Prometheus Unbound*


    Know ye not me,
The Titan? He who made his agony
The *barrier* to your else *all-conquering*
    foe?

        —*Ibid*


# XVIII


"'*Rock-a-bye, baby, in the treetop,*'" she paused to shift its weight, grunting, "'*When the wind blows, the cradle will rock . . .*'"

Mila held her only child close to her as she had so many times in the impossibly long twelve hours since its birth. He did not seem to require much sleep and she remembered what she had heard, or read, that only geniuses and total madmen failed

229

to rest. Many times she had eased him to his crib, only to see his blood-shot eyes fly open, wide and staring, just when she was beginning to relax her aching muscles.

And each time he had awakened, the infant didn't cry.

He growled.

Now, however, as she peered down into the face only a mother could love, Mila felt that he might sleep awhile. The poor thing, she thought maternally, sighing, he must be as worn out as I.

After all, he'd been steadily growing all night and into this morning. Now, holding him with the last residue of strength in her weary body, Mila realized with pride that her child was already the size of a three-year-old. A few more days, she mused with anticipation, if I can make him love me, and he will do whatever I ask of him. Anything at all . . .

Snatching a deep breath, Mila stood and carried him with difficulty to his downy crib. Everything was blue, as befitting a boy, even the rattle which he had broken in two in a snarling rage at four o'clock that morning. Even the teddy bear which rested against the bars, stuffing poking from its neck and the remains of its furry head strewn about the crib like animal litter. With infinite caution and a delicacy of motion one wouldn't have expected in so large a woman, Mila lowered him into his little bed.

"Up!" he shouted, his red eyes glaring lividly, hatefully up at her. His man's biceps flexed threateningly. "Get UP!"

Before she could conquer her surprise at hearing her child's first words, the newborn had clutched the edges of the crib in his long-nailed hands and tugged himself over the edge, dropping like a turd to the bedroom floor.

In common with all children, however, his effort of will was greater than his clumsy ability. At that moment, at least. The child's muscular legs wouldn't yet support him and he sat on his rear, hard. Surprised and furious, panting like a dog, he looked up at her with a killing expression in his red eyes. "Feed baby!" he commanded gutterally.

Mila batted her eyes in confusion and wrung her hands. She had striven several times to get him to take his bottle, only to see a hairy hand knock it flying across the room. Of course, the poor little darling must be hungry, but what could she do?

Maternal instinct took over. Mila caught a quick breath, reached down, and pulled the grotesque creature into her aching arms. Another inch, she noted philosophically, another pound. Turning crimson and feeling her insides suddenly shift hideously, Mila lugged it back to her bed and sank gratefully, wearily to the edge of the mattress.

"Mama's precious boy," she crooned, "Mama's

231

pride and joy."

For answer, the newborn grabbed her nightgown at the bodice and ripped it away from her immense, swollen breasts. "Hungry!" he offered by way of explanation, his voice bizarrely deep and insistent. His lips parted, showing twin porcelain rows of pearly-sharp teeth that closed avidly around a brown nipple. The teeth carved deep into the tender flesh and Mila cried out even as she stroked its incongruous snow white head, comforting it.

With its infant-sized hands, the thing gripped the teat hard, nails penetrating the skin. Soon it was making loud, contented slurping sounds. Traces of blood and milk seeped down its hairy chin. "Good!" he barked once, pausing momentarily to commend her. It even smiled. "Baby LOVE mama!"

Eventually it was through. Further weakened, Mila saw that it had grown still more. Its eyes were half closed, drowsy now, but she knew that she could not manage, just then, to carry it back to the crib. Instead, she rested the creature carefully at her feet, covering its peculiar frame with a blanket tugged from the bed. She was relieved when it stuck its three-inch long, prehensile thumb in its mouth, belched volubly, and fell asleep.

"What shall I name him?" wondered the mother, half-aloud. "Timmy? Billy, perhaps? Or what about Jerry?" The child turned in its sleep, its toenails raking her ankle and leaving a line of bright scarlet blood, but Mila didn't even notice it. "Perhaps something with dignity, like Edward, or Walter . . ."

"I was always so very proud, after I knew clearly I had been Demogorgon," Frank continued, quieter now as he leaned in his ripped pajamas against her pretty legs, "to be a part of the Bible. D'you remember *Genesis*, Lamia? Even in the story of Creation, well, I began to make my mark."

"I'm not sure I know the Bible all that well," she replied, a trifle miffed. "People like me do not ordinarily spend a lot of time reading the Good Book."

"I'll tell you what it says. 'There were *giants* in the earth in those days . . . mighty men who were of old, men of renown.'" He grinned almost boyishly. "In point of fact, darling, there was only one true giant."

"You?"

He nodded. "Old Caleb must have reported to his immortal leader Moses, speaking of the Great Court of Zeus, perhaps my greatest architectural accomplishment in Phoenicia. It has fifty Corinthian columns made of huge stone drums standing sixty-five feet high. They happen to be the tallest columns in the history of the world and they were a tribute from my people, to me." Now he turned on the floor, grasping her ankle. Again he was surprisingly gentle of touch, more than the man she'd known as Frank Triladus. He pressed his lips against her calf and she shivered. "But it was the last thing ever created there which is dearest to me, because I built and dedicated it to the most lovely woman I ever saw: Lamia Zacharius. It's called the Temple of Venus and rises nearly a thousand feet above the great acropolis. Think of that, darling, a temple built before Christ reaching a thousand feet into the sky!" Then he frowned, remembering, and released her ankle. "Yet you flew away from me to study at the sandeled feet of that—that fat old mathematician, Pythagoras!"

"How did you know you might find me in Indianapolis?" she asked huskily.

"When I was still sulking in the Himalayas with my sisters, even then beginning to forget my past, your vampire companion Vrukalakos informed me that he was going to America at Pythagoras' insistence. To begin Thessaly anew, near the Vale of Aphaca." He grunted disapprovingly. "Oh, he didn't tell me out of kindness, Lamia. I paid him handsomely for the knowledge, in Tibetans who worshipped me, because I knew you hadn't died and I prayed that you would go to America too."

"All those years," she said wonderingly,

stooping to lift his face to hers, "you sought me. Me."

He nodded. "It was hard to do but I adopted this—this more acceptable form and status in the hope of finding you and making you mine. My credentials as an archeologist were faked, of course, but I know the subject as few men ever knew it, because I lived through it all." He kissed her pouting lips eagerly, hungrily. "Have I succeeded, Lamia? Have I made you mine?"

She paused. "I want you as much as you want me," she confessed at last, eyes half-closed, "even if you are Demogorgon. But I am afraid, Frank; terrified of you."

Encouraged, he began for the first time to give vent to his eternal desires. His strong hands tugged her down on the floor beside him to kiss her mouth, her chin, the hollow of her throat, the warm place where her high and proud breasts converged. His fingers moved restlessly on the firm flesh of her wanting body until she moaned and then, acting from sheer masculine need, pressed against her.

Lamia blinked, startled by the extent of the pressure. Again his passions were overcoming his self-control, she knew. Again, he was growing. Her hand, reaching helplessly down with wonder, sent tremors of longing into the innermost depths of her; and yet she realized with clarity, as she saw his torso shed the remainder of his pajamas and the width of his shoulders expanding to double and then triple her own, that this heated way lay the worst fate a woman could suffer. Now his pajama trousers could no longer accommodate him at all and the wanting fingers of her clutching hand would no longer meet, would no longer reach even halfway round his throbbing maleness. It was, she thought with panic, like gripping the arm of a powerful man. Despite the plan formulating in her mind, Lamia felt fear suffusing her.

"Frank," she cried quickly, yanking her hand away to slap his cheek lightly, striving to gain his good brain's clear attention. "Listen to me! You must hear what I am saying to you!"

"Oh, no more words, not now my darling," he muttered, his burgeoning hands rendering her breasts the size of tasty walnuts. He could, at that moment, have taken either of them fully into his mouth. His head itself, though still handsome, was monstrous in proportions. "Think of the wonderful world we begin today, you and I! Consider how we shall rule this ridiculous planet together. You, with your intelligence and your psychic powers, and I with my tremendous power and leadership!" His hand was between her legs now, anxious. Though she longed for his touch, she knew that even his fingers might rip her asunder. "We will restore the grandeur of Greece, extend it to every city and village of the world!

236

You and I!"

"Yes, yes, we might," she answered with anxiety, closing his lips with her fingertips. "But there is something else we must do first. Damn you, Frank, listen to me!" She struggled to yank her lower body out from under his growing, painful weight. "You know as well as I the terrible danger Aether poses to the world and you knew it at the dinner table. Frank, we must stop *him!* It is our 'task, that which we must do together first, darling. Kill that ancient creature before we have no world left to rule!"

There was a creaking sound behind her of a door opening and Frank sat up. What she saw in the doorway made her reach out to Demogorgon for his protection.

No evil can happen to a good man,
  either in life
*Or* after death . . .

—Socrates


# XIX


Because of Mila Triladus' formidable bulk and
the amazing size of her glaring and grotesque
newborn, at the moment the two of them entered
the laboratory with a clatter of clumping footsteps
it would have been easy to imagine that the lab
floor tilted. Mila's face looked red from exertion
while her evil urchin, already as large as a four-
year-old boy but revealing the fierce, unforgiving
scowl of some ancient thing, held fast to its
mother's protective hand. After Lamia's initial
shock at seeing them in the doorway, she was irre-
pressibly reminded of an organ grinder and her
monkey. If one could ever peer, that is, into the
orbs of a harmless chimpanzee and see in them the
forceful, utterly mad intelligence which Lamia

saw in the eyes of this youthful creature.

The new mother had heroically coaxed bright red shorts bearing miniature Donald Duck heads over the padded diapers encasing his buttocks, giving the impression to Lamia and Frank that the thing was bottom heavy and might drop to the ground at any second. They did not know the effort its Capricornian brain put into everything in order to master things quickly and get on to its ultimate uses. On the child's feet were shoes it had already outgrown, cute white creations which it appeared to be trying to kick off with every lunging, purposeful step. Its long-waisted chest was bare, coated with a light, oddly pretty tracing of black and white down, like infant fur. And when it twisted to yank at its mother's arm, the mane-like appendage of hair streaming from between its pointy shoulder blades had kept pace with its general growth.

And now there it stood, several threatening feet from the lovely vampire, the sharp infant's teeth of its sloping, lower jaw lapping over its pallid upper lip, its nose well on the way toward becoming a piggish snout. It was having gas, but even beyond that it carried with it an aroma Lamia originally imagined to be urine. Then she realized it was worse than that, that it was a combination of wet clothes and the stink of turned earth after a night of driving rain—earth of the kind one might find in a yawning grave.

"Say hello to Aunt Lamia and Uncle Frank," Mila urged the monster, nudging. Its feet were awkwardly braced, like stones, and nothing happened so she pulled imperiously, maternally, on the baby hand. It reacted by yanking hard, this time almost toppling the big woman to the floor. Mila coughed nervously, righting herself. "They never do it when you want them to, but my precious miracle boy is speaking a little already so we came down to wish you a very - Merry Christmas."

Frank said nothing. Lamia murmured, "Joyous Noël."

Then Mila saw her incongruity, her narrow gaze sweeping to the ungifted Christmas tree. She flushed. "There was something else, too. We heard some ghastly news on the radio."

"How nice of you to remember us with it," Frank growled, rising at last to dust the knees bare through his torn pajama bottoms. He was himself again, in all ways, except for an evil headache and lowly taste in his mouth. "We have some news for you, too, my beloved sister. We're getting the hell out of this house you've just begun to haunt." He took Lamia's hand and smiled down at her. "My favorite assistant and I will be flying to the Himalayas tomorrow to record the origins of our little family. It seems I'm the missing link I've been looking for."

"Well, I could have told you that," Mila replied

archly, "if you'd bothered to ask. But you were having so much fun deluding yourself into believing that you were an ordinary man with a little memory loss that I decided not to bother you."

For a long moment Frank looked at the large woman, apparently choosing between anger and amusement. Finally he decided on the latter and shrugged as he dropped to his knees. "Let's have a look at your thing, sister," he said, making a face at her child. "I'd say you got more than you bargained for. Do you feed it coconuts or canonballs?"

"You're a fine one to talk," Mila snapped, "running around your laboratory half out of your pajamas." She smiled knowledgeably at Lamia. "It's clear to see that you've been up to your old tricks again. But this one seems to have gotten away."

Frank didn't answer. The creature in the red shorts and white baby shoes had begun toddling toward him, its knuckles dragging the floor. While he was utterly repulsed by it, he was fascinated by the enormity of its biceps and the uncanny intelligence banked like angry fire in its eyes. A yard from him, when he reached out for it, the white hair streaming from its head stood up like a mass of sharp wire and gave the creature something of the appearance of a giant cockatoo. Then, without warning, it flew into Frank's arms and began patting him clumsily on the back. "Daddy?" it cried. "Daddy?"

Lamia couldn't refrain. "What a charming family snapshot that would be, Frank," she observed with a smile. "Really, he takes after you in many respects. You're both big as a house."

"Thank you, Aunt Lamia," he said pointedly, sweetly. He looked down at the infant close to his chest, trying not to gag from the stench, and spoke to it comically, with a British accent. "Sorry, old luv, but I h'ain't yer bleedin' guvnor."

For answer, Mila's thing shoved Frank in the chest, hard, catching him off balance. When he let go to steady himself, it scuttled spider-like back to Mila. She held it, bravely enough, as it leered back at the archeologist with a defiant, maniacal grin. "Do you want to hear my news, dear brother, or not?" she asked.

"It's Aether," Lamia whispered, "isn't it? He's completely free?"

Mila nodded. "Free and out of the woods. According to the radio report, he's headed west on East 38th Street and no one has been able to slow him down. The death count is absolutely horrible."

"And the deaths were undoubtedly worse," Frank said, sighing. He looked at Lamia expectantly. "I don't see how this must concern us. We're citizens of the world, all of us. Greeks first, then the world. Why should we bother with one little city in the center of one nation?"

"You were never truly an evil person, Demogorgon," Lamia said, looking at him from beneath lowered lids. "Unlike Aether, you killed for a point. A purpose."

"Oh, I don't know," he said restlessly, searching for the remnants of his bathrobe and finding them too tattered to wear. "Aether has a motive of sorts. He's perpetually hungry. That's a pretty basic need, you know. If you look at it from his standpoint, thousands of years in a hole in the ground works up a pretty good appetite." He held her chin up to him to see her beautiful black eyes. "I know, my darling. I have a strong appetite myself."

"Make him see that he must help me kill the damnable thing, Mila," she pleaded, turning to the large woman with an earnest expression. "Help me convince him that it's his duty."

"That's what wives do, Lamia, and lovers." She was combing the infant's hair, now, many of the teeth snapping off as they cut through the tangle of premature white. "I'm only his sister."

"Precisely, Mila," Triladus replied, sitting on the couch. "For milennia women have been telling their menfolk about their damned 'duty.' Insisting upon all manner of outrageous things from fighting dinosaur to demanding raises from ugly little men with hearts of stone. Forever urging him out into the line of fire, into the hazardous jungle and the more hazardous city street, ousting us out the door into the rain or even a damned tornado, always in the name of 'duty.'" He saw her anger rising and raised a palm. "But hold on a moment, my sweetheart. We might work this thing out—if a bargain can be struck."

Lamia relaxed, smiling coolly at him. If he was dickering over details and agreeing to a bargain that would be met at some distant point in the future, she was on her own ground again. Not the terrain of a vampire, particularly, but the ground of any woman who knows her man. "Tell me, Frank," she purred sweetly. "What are your terms?"

Every city of any size has several streets which sweep from one side of town to the other, north to south or east to west. In the case of the immense monster from Antipodes, Aether had chosen to begin his unveering march on one of Indianapolis' east-west thoroughfares and was giving a new meaning to the idea of a street as a "main artery." Already East 38th was sticky with blood and, to the literal army of men striving to stop him, it seemed clear that he would break Indianapolis' heart in the most crippling sense of the word.

Aether could not know that the street on which he prowled passed a large neighborhood of middle-class people who labored for Chrysler,

General Electric, a variety of small stores and restaurants plus a command post of the United States Army; that he would cut straight through miles of shopping centers and automobile showrooms and apartment complexes before heading west; nor that his course would eventually take him within blocks of the fabled Indianapolis Motor Speedway and Indianapolis International Airport. Destiny wasn't something to which Aether gave much thought, like most things. Destiny was for the kind of people he was trampling or tearing apart, and he was satisfied that they were meeting theirs quite efficiently.

He could not know, either, what turmoil he was causing in three distinctly different yet closely communicating realms of humandom. One of those, the government of Indianapolis and, beyond that, the sovereign state of Indiana, was trying very hard to determine how to handle the presence of such a fearsome beast in its midst. The astute, affable and customarily unflappable mayor said earlier this day that the whole mess reminded him of crippling winter snowstorms a few years back. He remembered that event with fondness because he had been pictured frequently on camera wearing a gay little cap and seeming altogether heroic because of the way he had personally evaluated the weater conditions.

"I don't really believe there is a great deal of difference between the snow disaster and this one," Hizzoner quietly opined to his staff at the mayor's office. "Not in terms of handling it. It seems clear to me that my duty is to go *out* there, within a stone's throw of that—that monstrosity, and let them aim their television cameras at me." At this point, his eyes grew misty. He gestured with long, thin hands. "They can picture the dragon in the distance, you see, making it appear small, even ridiculous. Like a big tomcat, or maybe a lizard in the street. And with my reassuring juxtaposition to the darned thing, we can still city-wide panic before it gets out of hand."

"Mr. Mayor," began the visiting Democrat, trying to be as polite as possible, "I'm not at all sure you grasp how massive the damage already is. That animal wiped out an entire unit of the National Guard and every police official on the east side of the city." He paled, remembering. "Weapons seem to be useless against him, at least, conventional weaponry. Those that he didn't break into smithereens, he ate."

"'Weapons are useless!'" quoted the mayor, slamming the table with his palm, his eyes fiery with indignation. "Great Scott, man, you make it sound like something out of a Godzilla movie! All we need now is King Kong swinging through the woods to rescue us poor human beings!"

The Democrat looked thoughtfully at his hands. "That psychiatrist who's always trying to make the papers phoned. Doctor Kleinschmidt, I think his name is. He told me, Mr. Mayor, that one of the benefits of believing in God is that it teaches man to contain his imagination, to disbelieve in miraculous monsters that come out of the blue. He says ministers don't believe in the Loch Ness monster or U.F.O.s—until they see them." He looked up at the taller man. "And sometimes, when our imaginations have been stifled enough by the limited aspect of our faiths and beliefs, if we do see something we can't understand, why, we absolutely can't accept it. We try to deny its existence."

"I want to go out there," the mayor said stubbornly, "see for myself, and demonstrate the limitations of the animal."

"General Vanderleigh informed me on the hotline that it's damned hard to gauge how fast the fucking thing is coming," protested the vice-mayor. "It would look like bloody hell for the mayor to be purring reassuringly at the TV cameras at the exact moment he got *eaten!*"

"It is just this sort of talk," growled the mayor, flushing, shaking his long index, "that creates panic in situations like this."

"Situations," echoed the Democrat, "like this?"

The mayor ignored him. "I see it as my job to make the people understand they have nothing whatever to fear if they'll simply stay out of the creature's way."

"That's precisely the point, boss," said the vice-mayor, looking unhappy. "They have one hell of a lot to fear. Who knows when he'll veer off his course? Even if we decided to evacuate the city, these people are going to come back and find their houses smashed to kindling. Most of them," he noted dryly, "don't have insurance comprehensive enough to include damage by Dragon, you know. And then there'll be the old crackpots who refuse to leave and wind up being dead heroes, like that fellow Truman out at Mt. St. Helens."

"Not to mention what the miserable thing is doing to the streets," remarked the Democrat.

"The streets?" A glint of concern glinted in the mayor's eyes. "Do you really think he's damaging the streets?" He swallowed hard, biting the bullet. "Is he—is he making more p-potholes?"

His vice-mayor sighed. "I couldn't think how to tell you, sir, because I know the streets are a very touchy point with you. But yes, he's already ripped the shit out of everything east of Post Road."

"Ah, then there's still time!" exclaimed the mayor. He bounded exultantly to his feet. "Most of that territory is in Hancock County, not Marion! Bob, get General Vanderleigh on the hot line again. Tell him he has permission to use any means to stop that thing before it reaches Keystone Avenue—or worse, Meridian Street!"

"I think," the Democrat whispered to the vice-mayor, "that we just got martial law."

Meanwhile, two other exceedingly interested realms were having a field day with Aether's outing: the two city newspapers, and the three major television stations. Channel 20, the local public TV outlet, already opted to do an update on the disaster during the five minute break after *Mystery* and, if it was still hot news tomorrow night, cut into a Jacques Costeau show from 1973.

Press and television buildings alike were located roughly seven miles west, three miles south of Aether's current position and collectively had not enjoyed themselves so much since a rotund nutcase held a prominent realtor at gunpoint, live and on camera. They could see no way that they were personally in jeopardy and, in common with most Hoosiers living somewhere other than the line of Aether's passage, they had absolute confidence in man's ability to corral the monster.

Hence, the newspapers had been sending a steady procession of excited reporters out to the east side for days now as the editors huddled at their desks, figuring out how to connect the phenomenon to the Russians. "Creeping Communist menace" sounded good at first, since it might be said that Aether crept, and he was surely a menace. The symbolism of the thing crawling up from hell's red fires was also appealing, but the connection left something to be desired. With Jim Kilpatrick and Jeffrey Hart flying in from Washington, there remained hope that the tie-in would clarify.

For the people of television it was a time to shine and be observed by the bigshots at network level. CBS, ABC, and NBC were already getting hourly feeders, and the only thing which might upset the bandwagon, Indianapolis' TV execs felt, would be if Dan Rather refused to stay at his desk. Once Rather got the itch badly again, they knew the other nets would have to follow suit. The local boys would be quickly turned into official greeters and carriers of the spear, if that happened. But until then, East 38th Street leading out to Aether and Post Road was almost as chaotic, given its speeding trucks-full of television equipment, as it was at the source of the trouble.

Aether, the source, was finding everything a bit of a revelation. The creature gawked at the changes in human civilization over the centuries with all the zest of an out-of-town hick seeing his first skyscraper. Now that he was several miles from the woods of Thessaly and he had pierced the first—indeed, so far, the *only*—line of suburban resistance and defense, he learned to his surprise that there was very little resistance left. Now and then some fool-hardy members of the American Rifle Association came out and took a

250

few potshots at him, scurrying like mice when he turned to snarl at them. A gang of some twelve to fourteen muscular teenagers in tank tops and jeans stood in his path for a moment, screaming obscenities and pelting him with rocks and garbage. When his lizard tongue slipped out to adhere to the leader, than reel him off to his death, the others vanished in seconds.

Stoplights intrigued Aether, for awhile. Then he destroyed a few and learned, rather sheepishly, that they weren't alive. Automobiles and trucks left deserted along the road contained the tantalizing scent of warm humans, but after nuzzling and stomping a dozen or so, he came to realize that his ongoing banquet was momentarily stalled.

It was a clear winter day, no sign of snow in the heavens, and grand to be loose again. The immense animal was no longer starving for flesh and realized he had all the time in the world. At the corner of East 38th and Franklin Road, Aether paused to peer at eye level into apartments that were not always emptied. Some of these cave dwellers had either been away from home and without communications or deep in narcotic dreams when the sirens sounded and the word was spread. Now, going to their windows, they found themselves looking straight into the enormous creature's solemn eyes. When they began to scream, understandably enough, Aether contemplated ripping into the apartment buildings and prying the people out, like stubborn olives from a narrow bottle; but it scarcely seemed worth the trouble.

He had finally grasped the beautiful, basic truth of the situation, over the last hour, and couldn't quite believe the good fortune that had befallen him.

This was only *one* city, in *one* state, in *one* country. Why, everywhere he looked it seemed there was an abundance of human life! He'd been given a free pass to exotic, satisfying meals for an eternity and he would *never* have to return to the dismal life he'd endured deep in the earth.

A thousand years of dining on the finest delicacy of all, humankind, lay before him and he realized dimly that they would go on reproducing, continually replenishing the banquet tables without the slightest command on his part. He was the luckiest creature on the planet, Aether decided, smiling contentedly as he started west across a bridge. Several small boys threw rocks at him but his huge face was smiling when he turned to peer down at them. No need to lose one's temper, no need at all. Somewhere, out here, was lovely Lamia Zacharius; in the meantime, he'd see the sights and feast.

Aether waved his massive tail absent-mindedly at the small boys as he moved deeper into the city.

How will thy soul, cloven to its
      depths with terror,
Gape like a *hell* within!
            —Shelley, *Prometheus Unbound*


# XX


"I've finally decided to call the baby Dennis," Mila reported, putting him on the floor and beaming her affection at the gross newborn. "It always amused me to realize what 'Dennis' means when the name is spelled backwards."

Lamia reversed the spelling in her mind, glanced at Frank, and shuddered. The name was entirely appropriate.

Mila had given in at last to the baby's urge to roam, apparently unable to resist its powerful yanks on her aching arm, and now the creature was scuttling toward Lamia. She shrank away from it, warily, as it approached, and then saw that it only wished to sit beside her. Trying not to inhale deeply, she permitted it space and forced herself to pat its shoulder.

"What deal did you have in mind to strike with me, Frank?" she asked.

He sat on the edge of the lab table, self-conscious in his tattered clothing, and gave her an affectionate smile. "There's no question about our belonging together in either of our minds, I think. You want me, and I want you. Mila, here, has her new . . . son . . . to occupy her time, and there's nothing left to keep me in Indianapolis." He paused, lighting a rare cigarette and coughing a little. "The truth of the matter is, now that I must face the truth about myself I can't go back to Badler or U.I.L. to teach. It would be a sham."

"I can see that it would represent changes to you," Lamia conceded, still waiting.

"All I ask from you, darling, is this: If I agree to combat and destroy Aether—or chase the damnable creature back into its hole in the ground— you agree to leave the country with me. To become my woman permanently, for as long as we live."

Lamia hesitated, stalling. She knew certain things Frank did not know and did not dare confess them to him. "That could be a long time, indeed," she said.

"It could be forever," he admitted with a nod, holding her hand in his. "Although I am not immortal in the same sense you are, my dear, because I can be killed, I've never met anything capable of destroying me. Think of the delicious things we can do together! Think of how much more marvelous we can be with our powers and abilities combined!"

Lamia started to answer and became conscious of something in her lap. She looked down, startled, and saw that the baby—Dennis—had placed his paw there. When their eyes met, lovely black ones encountering red-rimmed orbs stretching to the threshold of Hades, the infant virtually leered at her. Offended, Lamia lifted the hand out of her lap and slapped it lightly. Dennis growled at her, flashing his fangs, and then slipped to the floor. Feelings hurt, he tottered back to his mother.

What she had not told Frank—somehow Lamia couldn't think of him in his historical guise of Demogorgon because she loved a man who seemed quite normal—was that he was wrong. When he drew the conclusion that she could alter her form, become a much larger being in order to enjoy sexual intercourse with him, he didn't know the plain truth. At the moment she attempted relations while in another guise, she would instantly revert to her own proportions and appearance. Therefore, the moment Demogorgon entered her—regardless of the beast she had become, or even if she remained a woman but one of towering stature—she would shrink at once to her genuine size.

And at that point his own immensity would simply gut her.

Lamia ransacked her mind for a way out. By invoking the magical soul-transplanting of *metempsychosis*, she was able to take full command of someone else's body. For a moment that gave her hope for them. But that left the question unanswered. Where in the world could she possibly find a seductive female body standing more than fifteen feet in height?

In a matter of seconds, then, Lamia was able to use her down-to-earth, deeply practical nature to face the plain, unhappy facts of the matter. There was absolutely no way to enjoy sexual relations with Frank Triladus. However much they might crave each other, the whole thing was impossible, unthinkable. Because she was not a man, Lamia adjusted speedily to the facts and weighed them against the necessity of destroying Aether.

Whether there was any sound reason why she should care about humankind or not, it was true that she did care. Oddly enough, it was at the moment that Mila completed the wondrous act of delivering a child that Lamia confessed to herself how human she remained at heart. The child born to the large woman was a monster, of course; but she, Lamia, hadn't known it would be at the time and she had longed to hold a normal, cuddly, happy little boy or girl in her arms. Perhaps it wasn't even too late for motherhood, Lamia mused; perhaps she, herself, could find a man without the past of Demogorgon who would love her and impregnate her. Perhaps she could persuade him to allow her to give him the gift of vampire-immortality; or perhaps, however unthinkable as it might be, perhaps she would someday love a man well enough to give up her own gift of eternity.

Boldly, then, knowing full well that she lied but doing it because her conscience was clear on the larger matters, Lamia looked steadily into Frank's face. "Yes, dearest man, I'll promise you what you want. Slay Aether, or confine him once more, and I will be yours until the end of time."

Just as he was taking her into his arms, Frank and Lamia heard the voice of Dennis, the newborn, calling imperiously from across the room: "Feed! Baby want food *now!*"

They turned to stare at the creature. He had come upon a bottle of faintly living flies and spiders in an experimental bottle belonging to Frank and was looking at the insects with an avid expression on his grotesquely babyish face. Then, in a flash, he'd figured out how to remove the lid from the jar and had his pudgy hand inside the bottle, snatching spiders and flies and poking them into his gaping mouth. Lamia's fingers went to her own lips in alarm. Frank started toward Dennis, ready to seize the bottle and take it away.

"That's all right, brother," Mila called cheerfully. "A baby needs lots of protein."

Hearing his mother, Dennis snarled, deep in his throat at the approaching archeologist as if to ward him off. When Frank shook his head and turned away with revulsion, the newborn filled his small hand again and shoved it into his mouth. "Good!" he shouted hoarsely, licking his fingers. "Yum-yum!"

Lamia blanched and sought to change the subject. "Without requiring sexual stimulus, Frank, do you still remember how to—to transfer to Demogorgon?" She laughed prettily. "God knows Aether won't provide you with that kind of motivation."

He considered it, frowning. "It's been so very long. I believe I can do it, though, by concentrating on an image of my own past reality."

"Try," she urged him eagerly. "We must know before we go after Aether."

He made a reluctant face and then reclined on the floor, feeling foolish. "If it works, darling, I'll never be able to stand up. Not in this room. I'd be far too large and cumbersome in such limited space."

"Don't think of me," she reminded him, standing and moving to his blind side.

He nodded and shut his eyes. A stillness descended on the laboratory room, unbroken except for the quiet spatter of snowfall starting against the old house. For a long moment nothing much appeared to happen and Lamia feared it wouldn't work.

But then, it did, without warning of any kind. It began at his head, where for an instant the Greek's skull was incredibly out of proportion to his form. He would never have been able to stand with such a swollen head, nor even sit up. Lamia glanced down the length of his body and saw the way his feet were growing, and then the legs. For a moment, she smiled at the incongruity of the giant head, giant feet and legs, contrasted with the archeologist's normal torso.

But her amusement swiftly turned to awe as Frank continued expanding, equally in all direction now. The remant of his pajamas peeled quickly away, leaving him naked on the floor before Lamia, Mila and the enthralled Dennis. He seemed oblivious to everything but his task, however, aware only of the superhuman effort he was putting into his remarkable growth. He seemed to himself almost to be in another world, now, a world in which all things were outsized and titanic. A slight humming sound escaped his wide, slightly-parted lips. Perspiration rolled from his massive forehead and temples, drenching the carpet. His pores began to look like cavities in his handsome face, each of them large enough to contain a fingertip. Now ugly Dennis approached, fascinated by the sight, poking at Frank with his tiny fingers and fists. The growing man gave no sign that he'd noticed. Instead, he went on adding to his height, his weight, his thickness. The peak of his head touched the far wall of the laboratory now. His feet began edging toward the door.

Lamia, however, wasn't looking at his head or his feet. Not any more. Her gaze had stopped almost midway up his body, staring at the masculine organ which he proposed to employ in intercourse with her. For a moment, emotions akin to penis envy swept over the beautiful woman, who treasured power and saw the thing as weapon-like. They were quickly dispelled by a hollow longing for Frank which her conscious mentality accepted as impossible, even self-destructive, but which she could not help feeling. By now, truly, Frank was Demogorgon, his height probably exceeding twenty feet, the monstrous instrument between his hairy, naked legs—flaccid against testicles the size of balloons—a good five feet long. Lamia licked her lips. A very good five feet indeed! What, she wondered, would it look like enpurpled and erect? There wasn't a she-creature on the planet who could take him in, she knew, unless it might be a female whale—Moby Dick with a sex change—or a female version of Aether.

She was quickly reminded of her original premise months ago when she set out to locate this enormous subdeity. That it would take great evil to defeat great evil. Now, loving Demogorgon's other existence as Frank Triladus, she began to doubt that he was nearly as evil as she had assumed. But the other parallel between them—their all-but-incomprehensible bulk, and length—was even more accurate than she'd imagined. For the first time, Lamia believed it was possible, actually possible, for Demogorgon to defeat the fabled beast of Antipodes.

And if he did, she thought as she glanced again at the incredible garden hose lying muscled but slack between Frank's powerful thighs, he would expect her to keep her word. Facing the fact, she felt a pang of terror uncommon to her. Could she even manage to get away from him when the moment came? Wasn't he capable, at his height, of reaching-up to pluck a Lamia-bird from the sky, strong enough to ensnare and shackle a galloping Lamia-filly?

Ah, if only he had been right! Lamia mused, watching him as he seemed to complete his growth and sit up. Vertically, his head reached the ceiling from his seated position. His chest and trim waist were oceans of rippling muscles, the Atlantic and Pacific set atop one another, the hairy patch at the center a tight-wound island in which Lamia longed to rest her head. It is not his limitation that prevents our joy, she thought, but my own.

Demonic Dennis was tugging at Demogorgon's oak-tree-arm, apparently wanting to play or perhaps test himself, and Lamia's amusement lilted. She was reminded of how much her would-be lover looked like Gulliver, resting from his travels, awakening to encounter the Lilliputians. Seeing the ugly child from vastly different dimensions of selfhood now, the giant easily picked the child up and set him in his palm, smiling almost fondly at the bizarre creature. Then, over Dennis' ugly head, he called to Lamia: "Well, dearest, what d'you think? Am I adequate to combat your mighty dragon?"

At the force of his words Lamia and Mila were both lifted from their chairs by the gusting breath issuing from his mouth and sent staggering helplessly away from him. Each woman caught her balance, Mila looking frightened and Lamia smiling her encouragement. "You're absolutely wonderful, my darling; *titanic!*" she replied with hearty praise. "Quite sufficient to handle any enemy in the universe, I think. But please, whisper when you're like this!"

"I'm sorry," he said under his breath, and the laboratory table and chairs quaked. "I'd forgotten what it was like."

She stepped between his sprawled legs, moved close to him and slipped her arm around the sides of his great head. "Once you slay him," she said gently, "I will join you—*anywhere.*" Her toes worked against his crotch. "At last we can consummate our desire. But now that you've proved that you can do it, I think it would be best if you . . . became Frank Triladus again. We cannot easily get to Aether without drawing a crowd if you stay this size."

He saw the wisdom of what she was saying and nodded. While he made the effort to shrink back to human size, Lamia saw Mila nursing the infant Dennis and turned away with repugnance. Not only spittle but twin canals of gore slid down her swollen breasts.

The last thing she and Frank saw before departing in quest of Aether was Mila, propping her new child on the laboratory table to change it. When she opened the diaper—they were downwind of it by then—both vampire and Demogorgon blinked and looked away. Only hours old, ferocious Dennis was built in a smaller scale of his uncle.

"Wave good-bye to them, baby," Mila urged the creature.

And Dennis waved, all right. He waved, nimbly, with his right foot.

Three thousand years of sleep-
    unsheltered hours,
And moments aye divided by keen pangs
Till they seemed years, torture and
    solitude,
Scorn and despair—*these* are mine empire.

Fiend, I defy thee! with a calm, fixed mind,
    All that thou canst inflict I beg thee
    do;
Foul Tyrant both of God and Human-kind,
    One only being shalt thou *not*
    subdue!
            —Shelley, *Prometheus Unbound*


# XXI


Operating as command posts have always operated at a strategic distance from the conflict yet close enough for executive orders to be speedily disseminated, the important minds finally decided to stop Aether short at a juncture marked

East 38th Street and Arlington Avenue. General Vanderleigh, clad in rumpled cap and rumpled uniform, drawing on an inexpensive pipe, did his best to look like his idol, Douglas MacArthur. Field glasses to his watchful eyes, he said without turning: "When the damned animal reaches us here it will be the start of its last moments of life."

The decision to draw the line there was founded on a realization that Aether's journey from his prior stop at Franklin Road would cover a stretch consisting primarily of businesses. Non-crucial businesses; expendables, if one wanted to take a hard line. But if the beast advanced westward of Arlington toward Emerson, Sherman Drive and Keystone—the primary intersections in his perambulating path—he would encounter more and more homes.

Part of the planning held that every business establishment heretofore lying in the way had long since been closed down with all employees headed, with enormous relief, for their widely-flung residences. But the houses beginning on the other side of Arlington Avenue might or might not be vacated.

Doctor Morris Himmel Kleinschmidt had elucidated his thoughts before arriving at the makeshift CP and found them accepted. "The American people," he'd said thoughtfully, "haven't had to undergo any seige or warfare of any kind since the Civil War. Not on these shores, with their own homes likely casualties of conflict. We are all conditioned to the idea that if we face trouble of any kind, we simply go home, lock ourselves in with a beer or a strong Scotch, and wait it out. We are not psychologically accustomed to the idea of going anywhere but home when we are in danger."

The mayor, who didn't care for behavioral psychologists, tried gamely to argue the point for several minutes. "My constituents have faced floods before, damaging snowstorms that crippled supply lines to grocery stores, and we've managed to move them out when it was necessary."

"Ah, but there's a significant difference, sir," Kleinschmidt had pointed out. "People *know* that floods recede, that snowstorms stop and snow melts. They know nothing about the behavior of legendary monsters, and I might remind you, with all due respect, neither do we."

"What d'you mean by that?" demanded the mayor.

Kleinschmidt shrugged and pulled on the rubberband he wore to remind him not to smoke anymore. "I mean that while Aether has followed a single-minded route and held to 38th Street all the way, we cannot be sure he won't abruptly decide to swerve into homes along the path and devour everyone in sight." He gave the mayor a dapper smile. "Some of his victims could even be Republicans."

The discussion elaborated on the psychologist's theme, pointing out that numerous residents would refuse to heed any warning and simply barricade themselves inside their homes. That might be adequate for most human threats, but considering how the dragon took apart the first National Guardsmen it had confronted, tables and chairs piled at a front door would represent a small obstacle indeed.

"For those among the lower economic classes, especially the underprivileged who are surviving at or near the zero subsistence level," Doctor Kleinschmidt finished, his attitude no less lofty under supremely trying circumstances, "it may appear that risking the very few things they have in the world—by leaving them alone and unprotected—is the final, intolerable straw. Portions of 38th Street, Mr. Mayor, are loaded with individuals of such unfortunate economic characteristics."

Once the decision was reached that 38th and Arlington would be the last stand for Indianapolis humankind, fresh units of the National Guard and several crack S.W.A.T. teams not only from the city but from neighboring cities such as Chicago, Louisville, and Cincinatti, converged on the intersection and sought to make it secure. Since the location had been among the top five "killer" intersections in Indianapolis for nearly twenty years, its annual accident rate relatively horrifying, some local folks thought it was a singularly appropriate site.

General Vanderleigh was officially in command at the scene and deployed his troops to the best of his ability. A discount department store roof accepted a squad of ace marksmen; a used car lot provided shields (in the form of scrubbed-up old Chevies and Fords) behind which mortar fire would begin; and the Carbob Restaurant could be utilized for an on-site CP as well as housing the next rank of troops which would be hurled into combat. The neighborhood Putt-Putt Miniature Golf Course was seen as an advantage of sorts, since it was absolutely level. A number of sharp-shooters stretched on their bellies in the snow, hiding behind toy-like golf obstacles. It would be their job to halt Aether if he veered south, down Arlington Avenue.

Heavy guns were for the most part concentrated in the middle of East 38th Street itself, to stop the great animal from continuing in its path. Should it turn north, to its right, other powerful armaments and teams using flamethrowers would attempt to force it back into the primary line of fire. And without knowing any of this was going on, or caring a lick even if he'd had a premonition, Aether had paused to investigate an all-night Haag Drug Store east of the selected combat zone. The flashing neon lights were trying on eyes that had been long-accustomed to the gloom of deep earth.

Towering high above the single-story edifice, the enormous creature gestured almost epicenely with its small, watchmaker's front feet, trying to wave the glare away.

On the other side of the drugstore, however, an automobile of out-of-towners had traveled southwest down intersecting Pendelton Pike without knowing the danger that awaited them. The car contained five teenaged boys coming to Indianapolis for a rock concert at Market Square Arena, and two of them had a thirst for beer to go with the marijuana secreted in the floor board of the vehicle. Only dimly aware that the neighborhood was deserted, the two boys—Ralph Sanford and Max Werlin—loped away from the car toward the abandoned drugstore.

It was miserable weather, the snow rising above their tennis shoes and soaking their socks. When they found the door locked, they rattled it several times with anger and took a step backward to appraise the scene.

"Where the shit is everybody at one o'clock in the afternoon?" demanded Max, somewhat less high than his companion.

"Maybe it's still closed up for Christmas," Ralph offered, doing one-hundred-and-eighty-degrees. A glint came into his small eyes. "Are you thinkin' what I'm thinkin'?"

Max frowned. "I'm afraid I am. Look, man, I don't want to get involved in no breakin' and enterin'. I just came along t'hear some acid rock."

"That's cool, man," Ralph said, pursing his lips and nodding a lot. "But look-it, there ain't nobody around at all! And that store has got to be full of goodies!"

"We'll find another store that's open," answered Max, turning to go back to the car. "I don't dig hot beer, anyway."

Ralph giggled. "That's a pun, ain't it?" He looked back at the locked door, glassed-in, sure to be responsive to one quick kick. But he wasn't thinking about the beer inside. He was thinking of the pharmaceutical department and drugs. Briefly, he glanced back to see Max climbing into the back seat, and then gave way to temptation.

His snow-caked foot went straight through the door and a siren wailed into the wintry afternoon like a lost soul. Ralph's eyes got big, he froze for a moment, and then shoved shards of glass out of the way and went into the store like a flash.

The shrieking alarm reached Aether's sensitive ears. Even monstrosities such as Aether can be deceived, and he put back his head, howling both in reply and mild pain. But a moment later he realized he'd been tricked, and didn't like it a bit. He took one smashing step forward.

The drugstore had been in his path and the foot went all the way through the roof, plus the counters and displays within. Ralph Sanford, suddenly finding himself in the midst of broken glass and sundered magazines with the low sky around his ears, looked about in instant terror. When he looked up, he saw Aether, looking down.

The other boys in the old car saw him, too, at last. Max started the engine as fast as he could and began backing hysterically away from the curb. But he was spinning his tires in the icy slush and making very little progress. Angered, Aether did two things. He snatched up the thief from the store, pinning him unceremoniously to his side for later reference; and he slammed his other foot down in front of the skidding automobile. Tires spun wildly as it collided with Aether's lower leg. It had all the impact of an ant dropping on the back of a mastiff.

Max gasped in terror out the window and up, and immediately found the distance between the beast, him and his friends, and the car disappearing at an alarming pace as they raised. When Aether had the car over his open mouth, he turned it sideways and tapped, almost reflectively, on its opposite door. The force of his blow broke all the windows and emptied the contents of the car into his gaping maw.

Aether closed his jaws, once. Crunchingly.

It grew very quite in the immediate neighborhood. There was the noise of incredible mastication and of swallowing. Then the only remaining sound was that of a vacated, old Dodge being slammed to the street where, at last, the motor stopped running. Moments later, Aether resumed his westward march.

It had been the first time Lamia tried mass hypnosis in decades, but she succeeded in her efforts and, accompanied by a Frank Triladus who remained his normal size, soon found herself through the lines east of Arlington, and in eyeshot of their monstrous goal.

"Dos Kodion, just look at that thing!" she whispered, clutching Frank's hand.

Aether was walking on all fours, now, indescribably large even at a distance. He'd been nearsighted most of his long life, and remained far enough away from them that he could not see them approach. In common with most very tall creatures, including men, he had a habit of looking first at eye level. Lamia Zacharius and Frank Triladus were well below that, the size of small pet dogs compared to a lanky basketball star.

They took their time staring at him. The impression they had was of some new multimillion dollar military tank outfitted with piston-like legs. At this distance, the scaly sides of the great beast looked metallic and impenetrable. When once he reared to look down on the roof of a building he was passing, Aether seemed fully as high as a five-story building.

"I want to try something," Lamia said briskly, dropping to one knee in the street and focusing her attention on the myopic, approaching titan.

As Frank waited, the lovely vampire's psychic extensions filtered through the lowering skies, probing for Aether's small brain, seeking to feel inside it and discover the monster's plans. When she made contact, at last, Lamia made a squealing sound and then raised her frightened face to Frank, clutching his arm. "His plans are very simple. He intends to dine on humankind—forever. He has no intention of living again in the Vale of Aphaca." Her black eyes were huge. "My darling, he's worse than evil, He is the only fully amoral creature I've ever seen. Anything he wishes to do is acceptable, he believes, and he regards p-people as the finest food he can eat!"

He took a deep breath, watching Aether come closer. "What else?"

"Most beings I've probed psychically have pressure points. Usually they're linked to what the being cares about. But with one exception, Frank, Aether doesn't care about anything. He sees himself as invincible and eternal and that attitude brought him to the point of having no other m-motivations but consuming humankind."

"You said there was one thing he cared about," Frank reminded her, watching her pale, anxious expression. "What is it?"

"Me, darling. He remembers seeing me, before, and for some insane reason he—desires me." She shuddered. "Sexually."

The archeologist's jaws set in grim lines. Flakes of snow were drifting over them, flecking his curly hair. "Is there any way at all you can attack him, psychically?"

Lamia shook her head. "He simply has no weak spots, no fears, no other needs. There is very little mind, to begin with." She paused. "It's beings who *think*—who are intelligent—who can be duped, deluded. Not brainless monstrosities."

"Then it's up to me," Frank said simply, soberly, rising to his feet with a sigh.

He took her into his arms, kissing her, holding her close against him. She responded fully, knowing, all at once, that if he lost—if Aether defeated Demogorgon—this might be the last time he ever kissed her. "Be careful," she whispered. "Please take care of yourself."

His only reply was to move several feet away from her and remove the clothing he had put on before rushing to the scene. Naked, an attractive man of normal size and proportions—a man whom Lamia could love, if only there was a way it could be done—Frank began his own feat of concentration.

This time the transformation was smoothly affected. It took a full minute, but he grew, expanded, evenly and steadily. And when he was at his mightiest, Demogorgon looked a long way down to the woman he wanted and blew her a kiss.

Even now, however, he was not nearly the height or weight of great Aether. It would be necessary for him to rely upon his man's wits and his human agility if he were to have a chance.

Lamia stared after him as he began his march toward the legendary creature of Antipodes, loving the immense musculature of his street-wide shoulders, admiring the narrowing of his buttocks and the powerful legs which took Demogorgon a block nearer Aether with every step.

When the dragon saw him coming, Lamia observed, there was an expression on its hideous face that combined surprise with something of reckless pleasure. And when Aether started walking toward Demogorgon, the very earth trembled beneath their feet.

At the precise moment they met, face to face, the giant Lamia had known as Frank Triladus smashed his fist into Aether's head with all his might. Caught offguard, the dragon fell back, stumbling. The man-thing followed up by another crushing blow with the other hand, dropping Aether to its back.

But when he fell to his knees and attempted to lock his massive hands round the monster's throat, Aether amazed both Demogorgon and the watching Lamia by simply shrugging him off! The man-thing bounced off a nearby building, causing several bricks to come loose and rain upon the street, unhurt but deeply concerned. If Aether were that strong off balance, what would he do on attack?

Demogorgon hadn't long to find out. Moving straight forward with incredible speed, Aether rammed the great human shape before him and locked sword-like teeth in his shoulder. The scream of pain from Demogorgon was like several sirens going off at the same time. Furious, he pounded the dragon about the head with his other hand knotted into a fist and saw the creature give ground. But when he reached down, intending to lift Aether and hurl him a block away, the evil cleverness of the beast was again revealed. Aether slid free, like a lizard, and fastened its many hand-like appendages in the man-thing's back, each great claw drawing blood that flowed to the street and turned the snow a lurid pink.

Demogorgon straightened with unbelievable strength, the dragon attached to his bare back, and began running backward with gathering speed. There was no building present to accommodate the size of them and Demogorgon simply lunged, backward, his bulk smashing the manimal into the concrete street.

The tactic worked. Most of the hand-like things loosened and those that remained were pulled out by the roots as Aether bawled his pain and protest. Instantly, Demogorgon whirled, falling on it, his mighty hands this time finding the monster's throat. But to Lamia's gasping horror, the creature simply opened its jaws wide and, as she stared, they began to close over the head of the man who'd been gentle Frank Triladus.

At the last moment possible, however—just as the piercing teeth were closing, ready to decapitate the massive human—Demogorgon found purchase and shoved up with one great shoulder, dislodging the beast and sending it spinning in an eastwardly direction.

Apparently confused, Aether began running away from them—back toward the woods of Thessaly, and the Vale of Aphaca—and the bleeding Demogorgon called out jubilantly: "We've got him now! He's on the run!"

Lamia willed herself to become an eagle, soaring and flying above her loved one's head, joining in the pursuit. But as she flew, she remembered what she had always heard of those monsters who were composed entirely of evil motivation: Distrust them when they try to flee, for it is the cornered beast that is most dangerous of all.

. . . For dream of ruin
To frozen caves out flight pursuing
Made us keep silence—thus—and thus—
Though silence is as hell to us.

For know there are *two worlds* of life and
    death:
One that which thou beholdest; but the
    other
Is beneath the grave, where do inhabit
The *shadows* of all forms that think and
    live
Till death unite them and they part no
    more.
                —Shelley, *Prometheus Unbound*

## XXII

Still waiting at the corner of East 38th Street
and Arlington Avenue, the military and police
troops were released from their hypnotic spell
when Lamia was, herself, well out of sight.

General Vanderleigh was first to see what was happening through his powerful field glasses and everyone could see him staring, his knuckles turning white, his trim body apparently immobilized.

"What is it you see, General?" asked the mayor. When he got no answer, he shook the general's arm and repeated the question. "Is it too horrible even to describe?"

Finally Vanderleigh lowered his glasses, keeping his face averted another moment in order to compose his expression. When he looked at the mayor and the others, at last, he was pale and wearing an insanely artificial smile.

"The monster won't be coming this way, after all," he said in a tight voice. "He's headed back to Thessaly."

"Well, then," cried Colonel Crowder, bustlingly throwing his rifle round his muscular shoulder, "let's get after him! Pick them off while they're running away, that's my motto! Take no prisoners!"

"Colonel," said the general, "Shut up. Just shut up a minute."

Vanderleigh started to peer through his binoculars again and decided he could do without that. His immediate problem was what to tell the others. And if there was one thing he wasn't about to do, it was risk a handsome retirement on the truth. How would it sound, he mused, to just blurt it out: I saw a woman turn into an eagle, and a dragon being chased by a naked white man as big as a mountain. How would it sound? Vanderleigh shook his head. He might as well check in with Doctor Kleinschmidt in the morning and kiss his command goodbye, forever.

Finally he gave an order and, after he'd said it, walked swiftly into the Carbob Restaurant to be by himself. "Make sure this position is secure," he commanded, avoiding Colonel Crowder's outraged gaze, "and hold tight. Just hold tight."

Later, he thought, he would take a car with some obedient corporal at the wheel and drive out to Thessaly to see for himself what had happened. If, that is, he didn't find the restaurant full of little green men from mars . . .

Lamia landed a few yards from Demogorgon and became herself, the image of the powerful she-eagle vanishing into nothingness. They were deep in the woods of Thessaly at last, standing in the snowspread Vale of Aphaca, and Aether was turning back to make his personal stand. It was bitterly cold there, the trees round them grey and white etchings, their greenery only a memory. There, to the left, was the shallow grave in which Pythagoras had buried poor Vrukalakos' torn remains; remains devastatingly created by the beast before her now. In the distance, poised in dream-like stillness in a clearing, was the midnight death-coach Vrukalakos had driven to terrify poor Mary Graham. The handsome horses, partly-mystical beings endowed with their own metempsychotic magic, watched what was happening with their eyes laid back in fright and their hooves pawing nervously at the ground.

Was it all, finally, to end here after all? Behind Aether she saw the opening of the rocky tunnels leading to Antipodes and the nameless dark things which dwelt with the dragon. There the brave folk of Thessaly had gone to certain death to prove their dedication to Pythagoras, their leader of three thousand years. After all that had happened since then, was she, the last vampire, destined to join the others?

Instinctively, she called up to her giant lover: "Watch him, Frank! Watch his every move! We're on his home territory now!"

Instantly Aether's bloodied head swiveled in her direction and, for the first time, he saw her.

Slowly, dazzlingly, a repulsive smile began to spread across the animal's fang-lined mouth. Forgotten, for the moment, was the annoying human titan before it. It had lost none of its confidence, none of its cunning. It had not run from fear, but for a better place to fight. Here, Aether felt, was where Demogorgon must die.

And here, he realized with a burning masculine need the creature had not experienced for hundreds of years, was where he would at last have sexual relations with the most beautiful human being he'd ever seen! And when she was wrecked by him, why, he would pay her the supreme honor and animate her to become his slave in Antipodes. His personal slave till the end of time.

Lamia sensed the change in Aether's mood and moved quickly behind one of her lover's enormous calves. The way that damnable thing stared at her made her feel grossly naked, and worse, helpless. In all the universe there might not be a dozen entities capable of frightening Lamia Zacharius, but she'd always known this dragon-like monstrosity was more than she could handle. She doubted that her teeth would penetrate his armor-like skin or be able to locate the jugular. She shuddered in fresh terror as she saw Aether lift himself to his hind legs and she saw, as well, the unsheathed dank member trembling like a tree branch at his center. If Demogorgon could not stop this beast, the same fate she had feared from him would befall her. But not in the arms, at least, of love and mutual wanting, but pressed like a bug into the foul dirt while this—this thing of reeking breath and oily, scaly musculature ground her into filthy nothingness.

Demogorgon leaped toward it—And Aether dodged, slithering like a snake through the great man's delving arms.

To her horror, Lamia saw Frank's massive head strike the rocky overhang above the cave entrance and he fell to his belly, the ground shaking. For a moment it seemed that he would rise, because he was shaking his head to clear it; then Demogorgon sighed and lasped into unconsciousness.

Reeking breath soiled Lamia from head to toe. Apparently Aether knew what she was, and what she could do, because he raised his many limbs above and around her, preventing Lamia from changing shape and flying or running off. His panting made nearby trees writhe; his dull eyes began to flow with a new imitation of life, a parodic yearning that was no less murderous for all its absurdity.

And then, with a delicacy of touch Lamia would have believed impossible, the vast and ugly male creature began slowly, deliberately, removing her clothes.


Deep in the cramped and baking bowels of the hollowed earth beneath Thessaly, the devil's demons and revivified workers of the monster who had abandoned them were having a party. For some of them, it was the first time they had ceased their miserable, back-breaking labors in thousands of maddening years. The penalty for failure to think for one's self and do what conscience-invoked logic insisted had long since stripped them of all individuality but for that of racking pain—until now.

Until these recent days when Aether rose like a phoenix to the earth on which they could no longer tred they had behaved as a single sinister organism, a smoothly-functioning, constantly-agonized machine created for the sole purpose of satisfying the needs of the great dragon. But, now, believing the master gone for good, they began reverting to the evil and soulless beings they had once been, tasting as best they could all that hovered on the shadowy interface between life and the grave. Demon and zombie alike, they cavorted in the subterranean chambers of Antipodes in myriad sin-filled ways that no ordinary mortal could have withstood watching.

A part of the merriment was that of near-ceaseless orgy, as if each thing had hoarded its lust through the unmarked centuries. Malevolent sprites and skeletal putrescence and obscene rotunds coupled in mindless ecstasy, using every orifice and phallus they could seize. Abominable slatterns with hair of fire danced wildly, exposing all there was to expose; masturbating pustules with festering organs propelled their husbanded semen into faces and forms; slimy anatomical parts separated in death from their fellows rolled and roiled, prodded and perched, crept and coveted, all with the cancerous call of death-music caromming off the ruined cave walls. A music of muttered madness, of overstretched license and even, occasionally, the pointless reenactment of murder foul.

What ghastly Things great Aether had dangled bloodily from the ceiling, to eat at a time of desperation, were crammed into starving mouths and promptly regurgitated by stomachs churning only bile and excresence. That which fell from their lips was itself welcomed by other bulging-eyed beings who fell to their creaking knees with moans of joy. An infected pool of stagnant water became simultaneously something in which to swim, even as other degraded and obscene lips bobbled forward dog-like, to lap, and served as a receptacle for stench-steeped urine.

When the shockwave of sound reached their ears, they all stopped. Listening. One by one they glanced in a frustration common to Hades at one another, some beginning to cry and while others smashed their fists on the unyielding ground.

*Aether*, they whispered with tremendous misery, *has returned*.


Demogorgon shook his head and sat up. What he saw that moment made him stare in disbelief and dismay. The woman he loved, beautiful Lamia, was nude and spreadeagled on the slushy earth, the vile and pitiless Aether poised above her body.

He ignored the pain in his head and leaped to

his feet, starting forward. But after a step, Aether's massive skull turned in his direction and the amused smile on the dragon's leering face told him the awful truth. While he was unconscious, his size had dwindled. He was once more the size of a normal human being!

Frank Triladus willed himself to grow, sweat popping-out like Indian beads on his forehead. Aether wasn't even concerned about his presence, hadn't even bothered to attack. Instead, like a monstrous spear head set ablaze, Aether's maleness was only feet above Lamia's unprotected form—and longer in size than her entire body!

Frank blinked, thinking rapidly, and knew there was only one thing to do. He must, like this crass and evil beast from the earth, focus upon Lamia's beauty in order to grow!

And at that instant, as if she had read his mind, Lamia sent her thoughts with urgency and candor into Frank's own mind. He would never know if she hoped to affect the change in him which he, himself, sought or if she believed that she was doomed and chose a fantasy to hold on to mentally at the moment she was hideously penetrated.

What Frank did know was that in his own thoughts he saw with perfect clarity the way it would be to make love to the loveliest vampire in history. It was in no way dreamlike; the visions forming in his mind bore with them every aspect of reality for him. He felt his lips suckling at her high breasts, heard her whisper wanting words in his ear, felt the dark nether hair between her legs and the moistness wanting him, opening to him. His body knew; his body understood that no man, at such a moment, wishes to be unprepared. Inwardly, in his mind, Frank felt himself entering her, sliding sweetly, lubriciously into the Vale of Vampire, touching only the Vortex, the only Antipodes he had ever sought. Her legs were around his waist, pulling him in still closer; her head was thrown back on the bed, the face damp with craving, the lips contorted—

And he looked down at her, a long way down, from a height so great he could not ever remember being so tall, so powerful. Beneath him, it seemed, the beast called Aether was little more than an alley cat who had snared a mouse and dared to toy cruelly with it. With one incredibly strong lunge, he had Aether's neck in the bend of his elbow and was lifting him away from Lamia. The man who had been Frank Triladus remembered, at that instant, one of his most magical properties from the long lost days of his youth in Baalbek. He remembered that he had been able to control the seasons, that the ancient people who'd worshipped him believed him capable of creating great windstorms. Hurricanes that swept everything in their path.

Exerting all his might, Demogorgon sighted the opening in the massive stone wall and bodily threw Aether into it. Before the furious, snarling creature could turn and clamor back to him, Demogorgon inhaled, and sucked in the air of Thessaly, possibly the air of all Indiana—and exhaled.

Tornadic winds lashed the woods. Trees bent, cracked, toppled. A wall of icy snow lifted from the earth itself, ripped away in one piece, and left the ground bare as the snow exploded against the tortured trees.

Most importantly, the huge, craggy stones around the Vale of Aphaca—some of them a permanent part of the scene for millenia, imbedded in the harsh winter earth before Indians bestrode the Hoosier countryside—smashed together round the massive opening and meshed as one. It was as if in seconds Demogorgon had made his own small mountain. When the winds subsided—when the air was no longer full of flying sheets of snow and ice or the pricking shards of broken branches—there was no sign whatever that there had ever been an entrance leading to the dismal, dark chambers of Antipodes.

Aether was trapped forever.

And the man who was no longer Frank Triladus, who would never again be the gentle archeologist because of the intrepid achievements of this day, turned like a revolving hillock of all-consuming self-pride and fervent lust. From the staggering height of his enormous head, a bellowed summons sounded like a death-knell for Lamia Zacharius. It was issued with all the command of a hundred-million armed and resourceful troops. "Come," he called boomingly down to her, putting out a hand. "COME to me!"

The Fiend lookt up and knew
His *mounted scale* aloft . . .
          —Milton, *Paradise Lost*


. . . And *Lamia's self, appear,*
Now, when the wine has done its rosy
    deed,
And every soul from human trammels
    freed,
No more so *strange* . . .
          —Keats, *Lamia*


# *XXIII*


Lamia struggled to get to her feet, shivering badly with her bare feet in the snow, acutely conscious of how cold she was and even more aware of her unshielded nudity. The snow continued to fall and her black eyes peering up at Demogorgon against a background of whiteness with her pale flesh punctuated by the triangulated sequence of darkness gave her the cursory appearance of a starving, wild deer. It was as if she were trapped here, flushed from Thessaly's woods by the shouts and screams of the bizarre combatants; but she knew the impossible truth that many hunters shot beautiful does.

More than anything else, that instant, Lamia was conscious that this was her moment of truth with the man she'd learned to adore as Frank Triladus, but whom she had known—though never in the Biblical sense—for tens of centuries. Both together and separately, the two of them had been incontrovertibly and remorselessly speeding toward this climactic moment for innumerable years beyond the lifespan of the longest lived, ordinary humans. Somewhere, she thought that instant, there is a faded parchment scroll bearing our names and this date, in this unfamiliar place in the center of a country that didn't even exist when we first met.

*"Well?"* the giant shouted at her, arms akimbo.

He had done all of that she asked of him—valiantly, and not without torn flesh and painful wounds. She could see the gashes in his shoulders and back where Aether had found purchase and sought the titan's death. He had saved the lives of countless human beings who would, seeing them as they actually were, have run in preference toward Aether. Surely he had richly won his rewards—

And just as surely, Lamia thought as she closed

her eyes briefly, he shall have them. Knowing that she doomed herself, but incapable of the final act of deceit which would brand her a traitor in her own eyes to the close of Time, Lamia reached up to touch Demogorgon's dangling fingers and nod. "Where do you want me, Frank?" she asked softly. "Take me wherever you please. The prize is yours."

For a measurable moment her eyes met his and a little of the old tenderness and affection crept back into his gaze. But the distance over which their eyes were obliged to sweep reminded Lamia, once more, that this gift of her own body to the man she loved was sealing her doom.

"Wait here," he whispered with a smile, the gust from his lips like a brisk breeze in her face.

She waited. Even though she thought of altering her form, and flying away to safety, Lamia waited by the Vale of Aphaca and the monstrous Aetherian tombstone erected by her anxious lover. And soon, to her surprise, he had returned with his massive arms filled with pine boughs! She saw unquestionably that he had deflowered perhaps a dozen trees in order to acquire these soft, winter bouquets. He knelt, without a word, to spread them into a bed on which they might recline.

His smile was boyish, not quite that of her Frank yet tinged with a romance that she found appealing. Fascinated with his preparations, she watched him build a circle of fire surrounding the pine bough pallet. The flames leapt high into the air and she could not imagine how she was intended to surmount them, if Demogorgon did, indeed, plan to make love to her at their burning heart.

Then, with a rather cavalier and proud masculine smile, he stooped to pick her lightly up in his arms and simply *stepped over* the mountain of flames!

Here, at last and at least, it was both warm and private. Teeth chattering, Lamia knelt as close to the blazing fires as she dared, briskly rubbing her hands together. It occurred to her that she could not wait much longer before her primordial need had to be satisfied—her need for human blood. The thought distracted her from the titanic man beside her; it served as a surrogate cigarette, and she turned away from him in a brown mood.

"My poor darling," he said to her, as softly as he could. Yet his breath nearly blew out the closest fire. "You have been through so very much."

She nodded. She felt something gently massaging her back and, for a moment, assumed it was his strong hands. When she realized that they were much too large for her narrow back, she turned slightly and saw only his immense, pink thumb stroking her between the shoulderblades. Despite herself, as she grew warm she began to relax—and began to want him.

A vampire always knows that her destruction, one day, is such a stern possibility that it is a virtual likelihood. As it is true of most worth-while things, the immortality a vampire possesses is only a sometimes thing, subject to the vagaries of living in a world with other beings. It was a gift precious to Lamia, yes; but it was also so precarious that it could be taken by failure to find fresh victims fast enough, by a smouldering cross pressed above the eyes, or a wooden stake driven—in the time honored way—through the heart.

Whether she could outlive the sexual prowess of mighty Demogorgon or not, Lamia could not tell. She knew it was possible that she would be obliged to live in sundered pieces, like Vrukalakos, in which case she hoped the giant killed her. If she was only physically wrecked, inside, it might be possible to find another female body into which she could force her soul by virtue of *metempsychosis*. But she knew herself well enough to know how embittering that process would be, how she would never trust or care for a mortal man again.

But whatever the cost, her man had won the right to it and when she felt comfortably, even sensually warm, she turned to face him and raised her arms. He lay on his side, for his face to be near hers; but even in that posture, with his head propped up by an elbow, he towered over her. As he lowered his enormous mouth to kiss her, he touched her high breasts with a great index finger, wonderingly, and drew it down her abdomen until it sought the ideal place between her lovely legs. Lamia gasped at his touch; she could not keep from it. A moment later he followed with his pursed lips and, when his face arrived where he meant for it to be, the tip of his crimson tongue shoved free to lap at her femaleness. Lamia raised her hips from the pine needles to meet him, her arms flung over her head in passion.

"You're so beautiful," he gasped, swift, hot breath on her aroused body, "the most beautiful woman I ever saw."

Instinctively, her hands went out to him and she closed her eyes. "And you're the most magnificent man," she swore to him.

But her rather small hands could not begin to encompass his penis and she held it, cuddled it, against her bosom, in her willing arms. Once she risked opening her eyes and had the impression distinctly of holding a skin-colored torpedo—of trying insanely to make love to an atomic bomb.

When she planted a kiss, however, the situation worsened. Impossibly, Demogorgon began to grow again!

Terrified, Lamia fell back into the pine boughs and saw the giant peering all the way down at himself even as his incredible shoulders widened and his towering head shot into the evening sky another full foot. A sound escaped his lips; it was the sound of someone in pain.

She took a closer look at his face and saw, to her horror, shivering white splinters—like cracks—beginning to run down from his hairline.

"No!" he cried with a bursting bellow so loud that two of the fires immediately went out. "I won't be deprived of you!"

Now he turned onto his belly, supporting the weight of his body by his muscular arms, fully astraddle Lamia. Looking up, it was like the sun had gone out and darkest night come upon her. Looking down, she saw the bloated mass of his manhood near her legs and quickly pushed them together, tightly. Perhaps she was ready to sacrifice herself before; but not now. Not to a man who was once more growing like a weed and whose erect penis was something she might have climbed in order to touch his underbelly.

"Help me!" he moaned, clearly in agonizing pain; and Lamia reached up to hold his maleness desperately in her hands. Relenting, she spread her legs apart as widely as possible and, her heart pounding in her ears, began guiding him toward the sweet orifice he had sought for two thousand years. His face was contorted with anguish and misery and yet he pleaded, "Now! Let me in!"

At the moment she tried, the other sounds began rising from the titan above her. They were the sounds of bones breaking. Bones stretched beyond all mortal endurance. Like thunder overhead, the cracking sounds reverberated in her ears, while her eyes saw the horror of millions of blood tinged cracks breaking in the skin, like a road map across his face. "I . . . did love you, Lamia," he managed to gasp.

And then she was rolling frantically from beneath him, the timing of her motion barely adequate. Demogorgon's massive carcass slapped the earth with the noise of a fissure forming in the earth itself. He stared at the Olympian heavens far above his astonishing height, then the whites of his eyes rolled into sight like twin snowballs sliding down the course from hell.

Breathing hard, almost overcome, Lamia again got to her feet and approached the dying colossus. His head was turned but every inch of his body which she could see in the scarlet striping of nearby flames was marred by titanic stretchmarks. Demogorgon's urge to mate with Lamia had overstepped nature's possibilities. She touched him in a light caress, then reached out to kiss his cheek. She was surprised to find herself weeping.

He turned his massive head a last time to see her, and smiled with no trace of Demogorgon left, just then; the terrible face was that of an ancient man whose most cherished mysteries had all gone sour. When he tried to speak again, the corners of his lips cracked, and something steaming lifted into the air. Demogorgon grimaced and an awful torn sound told Lamia that his bones were continuing to splinter with the muscles and tendons of his gigantic frame.

"Love," he commanded, gaspingly, gratingly; "even when you must kill, do it with love."

And when his eyes shut, the final miracle of Demogorgon began to occur. Little by little, accelerating with every decreasing inch, the giant corpse began to shrink. She stood back, unsure. And when the ghastly process ended, he was again the size and shape of Doctor Frank Triladus.

In the clearing, yards away, waited old Vrukalakos' death-coach and the team of mystic horses.

Lamia braced herself, legs apart, and whistled piercingly. The team trotted toward her, almost eager to be in action again, to be needed. For a moment, Lamia greeted each of the great steeds, stroking their muzzles, knowing that their valorous hearts were again ready to move, to run like midnight lightning.

Then she went around to the back of the death-coach, and opened the luggage compartment. With considerable difficulty, but less than with Demogorgon's, she dragged Frank's dead body to the compartment and lifted it in. A naked, black-haired beauty with gleaming tears streaming down her cheeks, Lamia Zacharius took the reins and called to her team. Silently, they trotted away, forever, from e soulless and murderous Vale of Aphaca.

. . . This is the law of God that virtue only is firm, and cannot be shaken by the tempest.

—Pythagoras

I see a mighty darkness
Filling the seat of power, and rays of gloom
Dart round, as light from the meridian
    sun.
—Ungazed upon . . . yet we feel it is
*A living Spirit.*

—Shelley, *Prometheus Unbound*

## *EPILOGUE*

She found the one-room church atop a hill— her *megaron*—fundamentally unchanged. On the roof, tilting at a faint angle after the winds of both winter and demonic warfare, the worshipful Greek Epsilon honoring Empedocles seemed to welcome her home again.

Lamia dismounted from the coach's seat, tying

the reins loosely to an *agyieu* or totem, and rummaged in the coach's interior. There she found the driver's coat Vrukalakos had worn and slipped it on. She was entering a holy place, after all.

She paused inside the door to hear the breezes whisking over the floor and muttering in the corners. A cloud of dust lifted, as if in greeting, and Lamia walked slowly down the aisle. All the pews were empty, of course. Every member of the Church of Mycone—the only church where Lamia had ever found peace, or felt at home—was long since devoured by Aether.

Gently lowering the heavy sack in her hand to the floor, Lamia took a seat near the front. It was easy to picture the Reverend Bandrocles delivering a sermon there, among the *korythale* or laurel leaves. Still standing at the altar was the *thrsus*, a focal point for prayer, and Lamia soberly inclined her head to it. If only that wonderful old wise man, Milo Traphonius, could emerge in the tunic he once wore as Pythagoras, in another day and age. Step to the altar and speak reassuringly to them of the book with all the answers, Empedocles' *grimoire*.

But there was no point in going on that way, Lamia knew, sighing. No point at all. The only way she could ever be reunited with her beloved *phrateres* was in dream, or time travel. She'd always sensed that a time for parting would come, one day, that she would need to be much more

300

adventurous and forward looking than her own nature made her. Because a vampire had to outlive all, forming an attachment even with a man such as Doctor Frank Triladus was an insane error. From now on, Lamia would permit no relationships of love. She would be true to her kind, and proud of it.

She placed the sack bearing her lovers' piteous remains beside the altar where, at least, the spirits of Pythagoras, Aristides, Andruss and the others would guard them well. It was time, this moment, to decide the course of her life from now on. And it occurred to Lamia Zacharius that she had more options than she once believed.

Somewhere in one of the deserted houses of Thessaly, probably the one owned by Milo and his wife, the magical book of ancient astrology—the *Bauernpratek*—awaited her use. Coupled with the skills of a vampire and psychic, it could be of rare use to her.

In the beautiful death-coach itself, she recalled, that devil Vrukalakos had assembled a virtual magician's laboratory. She knew that beneath its stygian seats, concealed in a compartment that contorted time and space themselves, lay wonders that the foolish modern world had never known. Surely she could learn to utilize them; and, if a universe of madmen intended a final war, she might yet be the one to stand between mankind—and eternity.

Mila Triladus and her grotesque creature Dennis, of course, remained in nearby Lawrence. If that ignorant but clever Amazon had her way, the brat would become a horror which only an immortal vampire might control. Thinking about mother and child, Lamia shuddered. What plans did Mila have for the thing, when she coupled with a lieutenant of Hades? Was it possible that Mila herself had some of the powers of her late brother?

And what of Joey Graham, the child whom Pythagoras once believed to be Triptolemus, the child savior of Greece? He and his mother, Mary, had undoubtedly returned to Indianapolis, but it would not be hard, finding them. Did young Joey truly have powers for the good? Latent abilities capable of becoming an antithesis to the horrid skills of Mila's offspring?

Feeling renewed and full of plans, Lamia Zacharius arose from her pew for the last time and went somberly, respectfully to the door. This time, she did not look back. She looked forward.

It had stopped snowing. The death-coach—hers, now, her source of intimidation and mystical magic—stood in stately majesty. The full moon rose above Thessaly and glowed sullenly in the blanket of new snow, and Lamia felt the stirrings within her. The growing hunger to feed. Drawing the coat tighter around her throat, her avid lips parted and one of the horses shied away,

302

eyes terrified.

First, the rites of restoration. A worthy victim, this time. Perhaps even someone to be vampirized. And then, when she was restored, when her uncanny powers were again at their most cunning and lethal, she would know what to do.

Life, and Lamia Zacharius, would be full again.

Empedocles of Agrigentum . . . spoke of two fundamental powers which set the universe in motion and continued to operate it thereafter— love and hate. These two principles drew things together or drove them apart.
—Benjamin Walker, *Man and the Beasts Within*

Declare the past, diagnose the present, foretell the future.

—Hippocrates

I write of things which I have neither seen nor suffered nor learned from another, things which are not and never have been . . .
—Lucian of Samosata

## YOU WILL ALSO WANT TO READ . . .